they

they

Helle Helle

Translated from the Danish by
Martin Aitken

akoya

LONDON

1

Later she goes over the fields with a cauliflower. Good-bye to those Kung Fu shoes. All roads lead to roads. She carries on into Vestergade, past the front-gardenless houses. A man waves from his breakfast. But when you come from round here houses aren't front-gardenless.

The tarmac glistens, theirs is after the square. Through the glass door and up the stairs. She lets herself in with her elbow, scuffs off her shoes:

'It's me!'

And again after that.

It's quite a heavy cauliflower. The sun stripes the floor.

They live above A Cut Above, hence the involuntary step cut. She puts it up in an updo, but half of it collapses. She blow-dries it with mousse and the mirror on a dining chair, she sits on her knees on the carpet. They always have wall-to-wall. It's a corner flat, it's not much to look at from outside.

The living room's painted to match a candlestick. It's dusty pink, but they never light the candle. They light it twice, only they discover it leaves a sooty mark. They sit by the window a lot, and on the settee, and with the free local weekly.

She comes back from the cabin trip with a wrong set of cutlery. Now they've got two-tower hallmark, engraved

IB. She puts the place mats out, she fries them each a fish. It's eelpout, they muddy the pan. Her mother claps her hands together. This is last year. There's no recollection of extractor hoods.

2

On the third of April her mother says:

'I must have swallowed a stone.'

They go for a walk by the playing fields, the anemones are out. Some small boys are playing football, shrieks and shouts, one of them's crying up against the goalpost. Her mother's in her winter coat. They're having beefburgers, therefore the walk. She's wearing an Icelandic sweater herself, it's too early yet, the wind goes through the wool.

'A stone stone?' she says, her mother nods.

'A heavy one. Here.'

She pauses a second and puts a hand to her coat, below the chest. They carry on then towards the pond. The shrubberies are dotted with crocuses, they don't care for crocuses.

On the way home they bump into Palle, her mother kicks up a leg in delight. Palle's from Clothes Man, sometimes he comes over and eats his sandwiches with her mother in the shop. In sunshine they sit with their feet outside the back door. He's going to see his niece and is in a hurry, he has a layer cake with him on the luggage rack. He turns and waves to them, the bike wobbles.

They don't talk about anything on the way home. Just before the square her mother says:

'I think I'll ask Palle round for a roast beef dinner one day. Do you think we should?'

'If you want.'

'It's not the sort of thing you cook for yourself, a roast beef dinner.'

She rearranges her room. The noticeboard goes over by the window. She has a number of cuttings and postcards and photographs. The cuttings are fixed with a single pin, they curl up from the bottom as the summer wears on. Her room faces the yard, she watches the dock plants grow at the foot of the rear building. The bin down there is full of hair. At one point a complete pair of plaits. She's so taken aback that she drops the bin lid with a bang and steps in some coffee grounds, there are always so many coffee grounds.

In June her mother can't get through her bread and jam. Normally she has a slice with honey too, and half a slice of white with cheese on top. The other half she wraps up and takes with her to the shop. Now she sits and drums her nails on the tabletop next to her plate, it's strawberry jam, she blows a strand away from her face. She really isn't hungry. But lots of people have no appetite first thing in the morning.

She herself shuttles between her yoghurt and the mirror in the hall, her German exam starts in an hour, she changes her shirt as well.

'You're flitting about,' her mother says.

'I need to get a move on.'

'Sit down, for crying out loud.'

'But I'll be late.'

'You've plenty of time.'

'No, I haven't.'

'It suits you that, just turn the collar up.'

'It's only you who still does that.'

'I dare say,' her mother says and looks at her plate, flexes her fingers.

One of the cuttings is from the *Politiken* newspaper, she finds a copy on the pavement outside the baker's. She's never been aware you can buy that paper at the baker's, and you can't, the baker woman says. Someone's had it with them and dropped it on their way out. It's from the day before, they study it over the counter. Tourists, most likely. She buys a wholemeal roll and often an individual butter portion.

When school breaks up the teachers put on a sketch. Her mother claps and claps, now and then she flaps the song sheet in front of her face, it starts a wave. They open the side door onto the fields. It's the emergency exit, they're not supposed to. Outside, everything's glorious green and blue. During the leavers' speech, in a short, breathless pause, first the cuckoo is heard, then the lapwing, and everyone laughs.

She has problems with her upcoming school bag, it's supposed to be a rucksack. But the straps are too short and they can't be adjusted. She buys it at the start of the summer holidays, she spends all her money on it. She's meant to be having a night out with Lone and Lone's cousin. Lone's cousin has left home, she lives above the old ironmonger's. She brews cider out of winter apples from their gran, she tells her they're for stewing. They sit in the cousin's little flat, each with a tall glass, and listen to music, they sing along, and when the notes are too high she mimes. She's not sure if the others notice or not. The cider circulates into her arms and legs, she taps her feet on the rug. She wants to stop dwelling on this and that. She thinks about the word noun, whether it's right. She still colour-codes her parts of speech, it's one of the things she's worried about going into gymnasium school.

Lone's cousin has a cactus collection under the roof window. They stand and look at it, identify the different types:

'Strawberry, banana, cowboy.'

When they poke their heads out they can nearly see the water tower. In the other direction the evening sun hangs above the square, a window's open in the flat.

Her mother sits in an armchair with the free weekly in front of her, she finds it a good way of relaxing, resting her eyes on the page without reading. The newspaper rustles, there's nothing she feels like doing. She's in her comfy clothes. Occasionally it happens that someone rings the bell unexpectedly. For that reason she's taught herself to glide about below window height. Her stomach rumbles and makes a racket, a fly leaves the arm rest. She's approaching a point where she no longer kills insects. There are some little green-winged things in the kitchen at the moment, she releases them carefully onto the window ledge. Now she gets to her feet, the slightest draught gives her a sore throat, it only takes a swallow to fly past. She closes the window with a bang, it echoes briefly in the high street.

Lone's cousin brings the roof window down on Lone's head, they fall about laughing, all three. They laugh and laugh. She gets the cousin's sock heel in her mouth and makes spitting motions, Lone bats the air above her head:

'Ow, ow.'

One of the tall glasses has been knocked over. She detects a long hair on her tongue and extracts it with her mouth wide open. Lone's cousin gets to her feet and rescues a cactus. She tries to get up herself, but trips on the corner of the rug. It all starts again from there, the sky's still blue. Lone lies sobbing. She's not going to gymnasium, she's starting an apprenticeship to be a cook. She advocates leaving the grease on cast-iron cookware. They're going to Step In, but no one normal goes out before midnight. That's two and a half hours away yet.

They spill down into the street to see what's happening. There's a bump on Lone's head. They pelt some signs with gravel, only someone comes. It's a man with two dogs, one of them's interested in Lone's cousin's shoes. The man pulls hard on the lead:

'Give over, Rover,' he says.

They sit down on a step and giggle. Once he turns the corner, they throw some more gravel. Lone gathers a whole handful. The air tastes slightly bitter, perhaps it's the cider.

Her mother thinks about wet weather, hail against a tent canvas. She's lying on her back in bed. A downpour in an allotment garden, potatoes awash. She stands in a crochet dress in water to her ankles, she's not cut out for that life. It's sixteen years ago. A brightening from the east, the baby in a carry cot on the garden table. She turns onto her stomach. When eventually she falls asleep she wakes up again after forty minutes every night. To begin with she staggers to the kitchen and puts some coffee on. This is back in February. She washes, even prepares a pork roast once. She stares at the black circles under her eyes every morning in the shop, reaches for her *cloud* concealer shade. One time she nearly snaps at a customer, it's not like her at all. She says so into the pillow:

'That's not like me!'

Then she smiles and remembers something she mustn't forget to tell. A car brakes in the street, she turns over again.

Lone's cousin flags down the town taxi, but there's a waiting list until two, a silver wedding at E4. Unless they're up for going now, he's got someone to collect at the ferries. Lone sits on the step with her head in her hands, in that case she prefers to bike it. Her cousin's not fussed. They can't make up their minds, the taxi drives off. But biking it's a non-starter. The cousin's is in Onsevig and hers has a flat. It punctures last year, she rides over a plank.

They fetch the rest of the cider, only it's warm. It's not a particularly good night for going out anyway, no one has any money until next week. She walks as far as the corner with Lone. They look at hairdressing prices, suck in their cheeks, then say goodbye for ever.

4

She sees the novel *Pavement Thoughts* as a brick of a book based on the observations she's made on her way to and from school over the years. The work's been in progress ever since fourth year, though as yet she's written nothing down. Now she makes herself comfy on the settee with a pad and a pen. She's turning into a coffee drinker, usually she makes a whole jug. It holds four big mugs in all. She sits with her feet up on the coffee table and the pad against her knee. She doesn't know where to start.

On the third day, a pair of pigeons settle on the roof. It inspires her to pen a lengthy rhyming poem about their clucking, she drinks two jugs before it's finished. But after that she feels unwell and can neither sit nor stand as queasy as she is, a strong upheaval in every hair root. She catches herself in the mirror on her way to the kitchen for a biscuit, her jaw hangs open, she's seldom seen herself so pale. When her mother gets home from the shop she's lying under the woolly blanket with the shivers. She watches tennis with the sound turned down, her mother neatens the windowsill:

'What a lot of cooing. Is there any coffee?' she says.

First thing after work every day her mother sets about the tidying. In winter she won't have her coat off before she's at it. In summer it's the opposite, she strips down to her underwear then as soon as she gets in. She goes from room to room, puts things back where they belong and waters the plants, clears the table.

She offers her assistance now and again in a timid voice. It's true that she leaves a mess, but she's tired herself after the daily grind, all this week for example she's a holiday replacement downstairs at A Cut Above, she starts yesterday. She sweeps the floor and performs the occasional shampoo and rinse. She enters appointments into the book and stands at the ready with capes. She wears soft-sole clogs, they're somebody's old ones. As they're cashing up at a quarter past six, she steps awkwardly, causing a detachment of the leather upper. She acts like nothing happens, puts them back in the cupboard. Cleaning for Annelise is better. There you get milk, and pears from the garden. But Annelise no longer has need of help, not now that the main office has closed. She sits on a stool in front of her house from morning till late afternoon. Her mother works in the shop before her mother, for which reason they always shout to each other that they're to say hello.

Apart from that, the summer holiday proceeds with one thing and another. She sorts through the photo album and bakes two kinds of bread. She looks after the shop for a few hours while her mother's in for tests. It's a quiet day, only three customers come in. One's a girl from the same year at school, she browses the lipsticks. She tries all sorts of different ones, soon the back of her hand's all pink. Her name is Janni. She wears a fringe and carries a proper lady's handbag. After approximately twenty minutes she produces a handkerchief from the bag, dabs her hand.

'Here, have a tissue,' she contrives to say, and reaches to hand her one over the counter.

'No thanks, I've sensitive skin.'

'OK. Are you going on holiday, then?'

'No, I'm going to a party. We're going to Norway for Christmas.'

'Well, have a nice trip,' she says, and corrects herself as the bell above the door, actually four little cowbells on a chain, ting-a-lings.

They're on their monthly trek to Holeby with the washing, the laundry's in an old farm building. They catch the bus from the bus station, it's Sunday, her mother's purse is heavy with coins. While the machines are on their cycle they walk up and down the street. She takes off her shoes, the tarmac's warm. Marigolds droop over the pavements. They walk out to the new houses and lap the estate, by then it's four o'clock and they hurry back. But their watch it seems is wrong, there's still time to go. They sit on the laundry table and play the ship is laden with, using a forgotten sock for the ship.

'The ship is laden with S,' she says, and tosses her mother the sock.

'Shite,' her mother says, the laundry woman comes in at the same moment, they laugh into their separate laundry bags. She gives them a punnet of raspberries for nothing, they walk cautiously, it teeters on top of the heavy washing.

5

They also live in a two-room flat near the wood. Here she becomes acquainted with the delight of treetops swaying soundlessly on the other side of a window pane. Her mother wants to celebrate moving in, she sends her to the Co-op for something nice. She can buy whatever she wants. She herself stays behind and unwraps knick-knacks and other items from the newspaper they're in. The carpet's burning hot, it's forty per cent nylon. Not that they've much more than the glass trolls and the Optimist. She gets to her feet with a table lamp, grinds to a halt at the windowsill. She'll consider crocheting some curtains if they don't become too fashionable. At the Co-op there are so many ways to go, shrimps and baguettes and warm liver pâté, she ends up with a tin of tuna and two rolls, she follows the footpath home through the wood. Her mother's standing in the window and waves with the table lamp. There's a rose growing up against the outside wall, it's yellow or yellowish, blooms until late July.

6

The day before term starts she insists they stay awake and go down into the yard around midnight. There's going to be a meteor shower, she hears someone mention it. Her mother brings a cushion. Unfortunately the yard is partially illuminated by a floodlight at the beer depot. Her mother lies down immediately on the cement with her head on the cushion, she folds her hands on top of her chest, her face glistens with night cream:

'That's aeroplanes,' she says.

'It hasn't started yet.'

There's a rustling under the dock plants, the only other sound is an electric hum. She stands with her arms at her sides, head tipped back. The floodlight at the depot goes out.

'Wake me at half past seven,' her mother says.

'Can't you shut up for two minutes? Besides, the bus goes at quarter past,' she says.

'From Rødbyhavn?'

'No, that's where it comes from.'

'That's what I thought,' her mother says, and a moment later:

'You'll be dead excited.'

'Yes, Mum,' she says in block capitals, now something's happening in the left of her visual field, but then the depot light comes on again, someone clears their throat meticulously behind the fence.

The next morning there's grit in her eyes. Cold

water helps, and time, and thinking about something else. She thinks about the fly in the windowsill, what it's going to decide on after the apple.

7

Her mother falls into a reverie with the hairspray. She goes nearly all the way to Karleby in a sidecar once, her flapping scarf. The trees are yellows and reds. They mistake withered leaves in a farmyard for scampering mice. The air can be so fresh in autumn, without all that dust from flowers and herbaceous borders. A disagreement takes place, she insists on cold food, she'll be party to nothing else. She gets out, walks the rest of the way along a disused railway line. Her shoes she carries. She won't say she doesn't want it any other way. But she's not equipped to manage the sudden change to the everyday. Squabbling over an eel. Silence. If that's how it's going to be, she prefers to be on her own, but she isn't on her own.

8

The town has 2,572 inhabitants. And yet she's never seen Tove Dunk. Tove wears a lamb's leather vest, she uses the word *lunch*. Every morning on the bus she can hear Tove's alto at the back. She herself occupies a seat in the middle with her knees wedged against the back of the one in front, she gazes out at houses and farms.

It's late August, it's raining. People get on at bus stops and the ends of gravel tracks, they say their good mornings as they pass through the aisle. From Hillested the seat is no longer her own, a girl from Y sits down beside her, her long hair drips.

'Oh, sorry,' she says.

'It's all right.'

'I've just washed it. Thank goodness I didn't dry it.'

'You have to get lucky sometimes.'

'Sounds about right.'

'It's what you make of it.'

The girl produces a plastic box from her bag:

'Do you want a grape?'

'No thanks.'

'Are you fasting?'

'No.'

'Oh, OK. I thought you were the girl who hung out with Tove Dunk.'

Before they reach the bus station the weather clears. They make their way towards the school in dribs and drabs, she sticks with two boys from Ahornvej, they know each other from once. But at the shopping centre the boys carry on towards the newsagent's. She stops a moment, asks herself if she's brought any money with her, but she hasn't. On her way through the centre concourse she bypasses a very large puddle. Tove Dunk overtakes on the opposite bank, flaps a hand in front of her face:

'Phew, what a humid day,' she says.

They both smile, continue neck and neck past the pub. As they cross the car park outside, Tove Dunk says:

'Hold this a sec, will you?'

She hands her her bag, divests herself of her raincoat. She's wearing a striped shirt with gold threads under her leather vest, she adjusts the way it sits.

'Thanks for the help, brilliant,' she says.

There's two minutes until the bell. They speed up, neither of them speaks the last bit of the way. In front of the main building she hears herself say:

'I'm fasting.'

But then the door opens, it's the music teacher with a mug and a vacuum jug:

'Ladies,' he says, Tove Dunk smiles:

'See you,' she says, and lifts two fingers.

The same day there's a students' meeting in the break, concerning the obtaining of a drinks machine. It takes place in a disorderly basement room called the canteen. The student in charge of the meeting sits cross-legged on top of a table, though rumour has it she's a conservative. They're to make a decision as to cold or hot drinks. Moreover, a drinks-machine link person is to be elected, alternatively a rota schedule established. But this involves a certain risk, in view of the sizeable sums of money a drinks machine may often contain. A debate ensues. A young man in desert boots shakes his head a number of times. Another tips over backwards on his chair and lands on a heap of sports bags, confusion and uproar.

On the way back to their demountable she spots the one in the desert boots, he's standing on the grass with a small group of others. They're third years, they take turns to bite from a loaf. Just as she's passing, one of them says:

'They're undermining themselves.'

To which Desert Boots replies:

'It's totally abstract.'

She sits beside Hafni in maths. Hafni carries her books in a basket, she wears harem pants. She's kind enough to write results down on a little notepad even before you ask. Hafni has a crush on someone from Z, they have Russian together. She falls head over heels for him in their first lesson because of his hair. Plus the poster tube that's always sticking up out of his rucksack, Hafni's in a lather about it:

'It's giving me stomach aches, I'm going to fail,' she says whilst rearranging her basket. She puts every-thing out onto the table after the lesson, then puts it all back again. Now it's PE, they walk together to the changing room. Hafni wants to go for a run like they did last time, the teacher consents. They run through the shopping centre to the health shop. They look at teas and nettle soap, then they run into Frellsen's for soft serve. They eat under a tree.

Last lesson of the day is history. She sits at the back and writes a list of things she wants to change about herself. Perhaps she'll buy an old pea coat, she considers taking up painting too. The history teacher sports a denim skirt, she stands with her glasses in her hand. Whenever she asks a question she puts on her glasses and scans the class. They talk about feudal society, the history teacher draws a graph on the board, her hair's styled with an undercut at the nape. Now the sky is blue above the big roof windows. The teacher turns again, puts on her glasses:

'What characterises the commoners, come on?' she says, and dips at the knees.

For some reason she feels an urge to answer without raising a finger first:

'It's totally abstract,' she says, the history teacher tilts her head, knees still bent:

'All right. In what way?' she says, but then fortunately someone sends a packet of Digestives round.

On her way to the station she endeavours to extract her sandwiches from her bag. But when she turns down after the high street Tove Dunk is standing up ahead on top of a boulder. A pair of second years are sat on the grass at her feet. She lets the sandwiches slip back straight away into her bag, walks on at a normal pace along the opposite pavement. Tove Dunk catches sight of her and shouts:

'Do you want to come with us to Hot Beets?'

'Hot what?' she says as she crosses over, no one hears.

'It's good you came,' Tove Dunk says, and jumps down.

The others get up and together they walk the rest of the way to the bus.

9

On Poppelvej they have a sideboard with a mirror and a bar cabinet. They put a bottle of mulled wine in it. They use the mirror to do their hair in, if the other mirror is occupied. It doesn't really agree with them living in a housing estate house, the doors are made of cardboard. She goes to shut one with her heel and her heel goes right through. Her mother washes her feet in the sink and the sink comes off the wall. She catches it halfway, it's an awkward manoeuvre, her foot considering. The owner thinks it better they move again. The house is to be rented out now to a widower, he comes and views. Her mother boils cod roe the evening before. But then he has a poinsettia with him, and his jacket's far too big. Moreover, he thinks at first there's an extra room behind the sideboard because of the mirror. They pretend not to be aware of his mistake, even when it dawns on him. Her mother ushers him into the bedroom, demonstrates the roller blind. He talks about the bed as if it's included in the let, he lies down on it. They hurry back out, not looking at each other until he gets in his car again, or perhaps when he bangs the car door shut.

10

Every day her mother enjoys an interlude on the step when the high street's quiet and the afternoon sun touches the electrical suppliers. A dog sits waiting on its lead. It's her eighth year in the shop, she's entrusted with nearly everything, from layout to stock. She's even granted a course in signwriting, but she refuses to write *pantyhose*. She wipes the racks and polishes the glass-topped counter and steps outside leaving the door open behind her. Looks up and down the street. Not a soul but for the baker woman's back. She fills her mouth with air and holds her nose. Increasingly, she experiences a rushing sound in one ear, moreover an occasional reverb when she speaks.

'It's like there's a resonance inside my head,' she says when they sit down to the aforementioned roast beef.

'I thought I could hear something funny,' Palle says, and loses control of his saliva, the gravy sloshes, their laughter swells, they crease up and collapse over the table, they must all three sit wiping their eyes for some time before they can eat anything at all. It's because of the pills, it's a side effect. The blockage in her right ear now clears, the sun stripe shifts a smidgeon. There's life in the street again, an elderly couple trundle out of the Co-op, the dog gets up.

She gets something in her eye just after the bus station, puts her school bag down on a bench and picks it out. Lifts and lowers her shoulders, she's wearing the wrong clothes today, in the breaks she keeps pulling and pulling at her cropped jumper, until Hafni takes her arm:

'You're driving me up the wall!'

'You can see my stomach.'

'What stomach?' Hafni says, and partly on that account she swerves a moment later from the bus station into the Co-op and buys a nutty nougat bar. On her way out she sees someone from her old school coming towards the entrance, avoids them by probing into both bag and eye, canters across the street and into the shop:

'It's me!'

'Hello you,' her mother calls from the back room, and a couple of minutes later, after they've stood with some cardboard hangers and she wants to get home with her nougat:

'Chow, chow.'

To this as usual she gives no reply, only a very measured backward wave over her shoulder.

11

She's going for evening tea at Tove Dunk's. From the road outside she can see her parents doing the dishes, the window's open, the radio's on. They're newcomers here, her dad holds a high position in the local authority. He waves to her with the tea towel. She waits on the step, doesn't know whether to knock. Some time elapses. Their names are all on the door. At last it opens, it's Tove in an orange skirt.

'Come in, it's a hand-me-down from my mum,' she says.

She makes to remove her Kung Fu shoes, but Tove shakes her head. The boiler kicks in, Tove makes a face. They go through the living room and out onto the patio, the sun hangs low behind some tall spruce trees at the bottom of the garden. Tove's father says hello from the patio door, her mother calls a hi over his shoulder. The television goes on. The air is cool, there's a smell of fermented fallen fruit. Tove's put mugs and milk on the outside table, they sit down.

'No, let's make the tea at once,' Tove then says, and so they get to their feet again, go back through the living room, pass behind her seated parents. In the kitchen, two tea towels are drying on the radiator. The kettle's apparently already boiled, Tove fills the tea pot. She opens a cupboard:

'Do you like brie with honey?'

'I think so.'

'We'll have some crispbread then.'

'OK.'

'There's crispbread,' Tove's mother shouts very loudly from the living room, Tove raises her eyebrows:

'Thank you,' she shouts back just as loudly, bonks a teaspoon against her forehead. They go back through the living room with tray and teapot respectively, Tove's parents with their backs to them in the corner of the sofa, her mother with her head on her father's shoulder.

'Can't you turn it down a bit, we can hardly hear ourselves think,' Tove says as they go out, and a moment later when they sit down at the table:

'Fuddy-duddies.'

They both begin to laugh then, Tove's laughter is bubbly and rather drawn out, they laugh and laugh, also because there's only water in the tea pot, and because of the brie. After several minutes, Tove's mother appears in the doorway smiling:

'What are you up to?' she says, and they laugh only slightly more then.

Shortly before eight there's a knock on the carport. It's Desert Boots and someone called Bob. They've biked over from Gerringe, they've brought beers in a carrier bag. Plus plums from somewhere on the way, many are a bit squashed on account of the beer bottles. They sit down at the table outside. Bob lights a cigarette, he blows the smoke at the midges. After a bit, Tove's mother's in the doorway again:

'You should come inside now or you'll catch your death,' she says.

'Care for a plum?' says Bob.

'Don't mind if I do,' she says and steps down to take one. She stands and eats it at the end of the table.

'They're very good,' she says.

'They're from just before Nebbelunde,' says Bob.

'From the ceramic artists?' she says.

'No, just from a tree,' says Bob.

'We'll be in in a minute,' Tove says, and her mother nods, she's still got plum in her mouth:

'Mmm,' she says.

They remain at the table, an hour and a half goes by. Her beer bottle's clasped in her hands getting colder and colder. Tove's teeth chatter a few times, Bob appears unaffected by the temperature. He leans into the table with his beer number three, takes small, measured swigs. Then eventually they agree it's too cold and everyone gets up. Tove takes the tray and the others follow with beer and cushions. But now the patio door is locked and they have to go in through the hall.

'Just dump the cushions there,' Tove says with a nod towards the boiler room, she carries on through into the kitchen, Bob goes to the toilet.

'Where do you think she means?' says Desert Boots, his name is Steffen.

'There maybe,' she says, and he puts them on top of a shoe rack, they go down the hall and look into a room, only it's not Tove's. Then Tove comes back with a shawl around her shoulders, she opens the door of the room that's hers and switches the ceiling light on, switches it off again quickly, digs out some candles.

The beers are mixed up, they don't know whose is whose. Bob holds a bottle in the air, the label's been shredded:

'Who's the nervous one?' he says, the beer is hers,

she holds her hand out and takes it, downs a swig. They sit for a bit without saying much. Bob revolves on his chair and examines the records on the shelf, pulls out an LP, holds it up in front of him. Tove goes to the toilet. A band of light falls across Steffen's legs, he's sat with them crossed. He keeps looking her in the eye. Tove says something in the hall, her dad replies.

At quarter to eleven they break up. Tove sees them out to the road, she's still got the shawl on. They agree to go together to the opening of a book café in Nakskov in two weeks' time, all three are in the support association. She can join too if she wants, it costs twenty kroner. Steffen might have some payment forms at home. There isn't a breath of wind, the sky is black and filled with stars. Bob jumps on his bike. Steffen rummages in his pocket, plonks himself down on the luggage rack. Reaching the corner they shout:

'See you!'

'Thanks for a lovely time!'

'Sleep well! Thanks for the beer,' Tove shouts from her drive.

She for her part is already a short way along the pavement, she stops a moment and turns:

'Yes, thanks for the brie,' she shouts, just before Tove's door closes.

12

At the crossroads they acquire a new settee. It's one that's for sale as used, only it hasn't actually been used. It's red velour with tassels. They put it in front of the window, a rat finds its way in and scurries behind the tassels. It's over from the hotel, her mother succeeds in chasing it out. But from now on they'll sleep with shovels. When a lorry turns the corner it looks like it's on its way into the living room. One of the drivers waves with his cigarette. It's the same one who helps them with their next move, he shifts nearly the whole lot on his own. Despite this, they can never remember his name, Holger or something.

The leisure learning season starts in week 38. She enrolls them on the course herself, it's called *Life and its Philosophy*. It takes place in her old classroom, the teacher's one Per Tønnesen. Her mother wears her white shirt and pleated trousers. They're too big for her now, but she won't throw them out, especially not after that business with Bruno. He presents himself last week as she's on her way from the shop, he presents himself far too often altogether. She's standing with the day's takings at the night safe, all of a sudden he comes up behind her:

'Can I tell you one thing honestly, my dear? Those trousers have gone baggy at the seat, they used to fit you so well.'

She turns slowly, an icy cold runs through her arms and legs, all the way into her handbag in fact:

'What am I supposed to say to that, Bruno?' she says and takes a deep breath, marches away along the pavement as resolutely as high heels and body weight allow, loosens her hips demonstratively after passing Acacia, she senses him still staring.

Unfortunately, the course looks like it can't go ahead due to lack of interest, there are only four enrolments. The two others are a married couple from Nysted, the woman's blind. Per Tønnesen sits behind the teacher's desk with the list. They must wait and see if anyone else comes at the last minute. Her mother studies a cluster of little holes in the desktop, they're from a pair of compasses.

'They're from a pair of compasses,' she says.

'Aah,' her mother says.

'What are?' the blind woman says.

'In the desktop,' her husband says.

'I know because this is my old classroom,' she hears herself say in an unfamiliar adult voice, she pronounces every syllable meticulously. But the woman hears perfectly well. Her mother smiles at the couple:

'We live here in town,' she says and points through the window.

'Oh, I see,' says the man.

'Oh,' says the woman with a nod.

'But Nysted's a lovely place too,' her mother says, and they all nod then except Per Tønnesen, he sits with his hands behind his head, the sleeves of his checked jacket ride up his forearms.

Her new way of talking continues nearly an hour. Although the course won't go ahead it seems wrong to just get up and go. They chat about various topics prompted by the title.

'It so happens I work in the field myself,' the man says.

He's a travel guide in his spare time, they're away nearly every holiday. Among other places they've been to Madeira no fewer than eleven times.

'When my wife was sighted she organised the hikes,' he says, they all nod again, Per Tønnesen with his chin propped in his clenched hand. A water pipe whistles, someone turns the tap on downstairs in the staff kitchen. She leans forward, looks across at the woman:

'It must be a great loss,' she says.

'You learn to live with it,' the woman says.

'Is it better to be born blind, I wonder? At least then you don't know what you're missing,' her mother says, now Per Tønnesen stirs, he clears his throat, but says nothing.

'Yes, that's the big question,' the husband says, her mother expels a thoughtful sound, looks up at the ceiling.

She herself straightens up on her chair:

'Whoever has seen a sunrise will always carry it with them in their inner being,' she says, they look at her all at once, the blind woman nods emphatically.

Not long afterwards they scrape away from the desks and shrug on their coats, utter thanks and all the bests, a shame it's just the once. Her mother puts an arm around her on the stairs:

'So well spoken you are, and only sixteen.'

'Not now, Mum,' she says, and extricates herself, a bunch of keys rattles at their rear, it's Per Tønnesen.

'A shame it was just the once,' he says, her mother turns:

'It was very interesting all the same.'

'Glad to hear it,' he says from somewhere in his beard, he turns out to be quite a tall man.

'Interesting people, interesting evenings, isn't that what they say?' her mother says with a laugh, Per Tønnesen laughs too, they stand a moment laughing on the staircase, fortunately the married couple now emerge onto the landing above them and some fuss occurs regarding the banister and their impending descent.

'I'm not sure it was our sort of thing really,' her mother says as they cross the square, the drizzle hangs under the street lighting, a car pulls away, then another, and the town is still again.

14

For a very short period they live in half a house near Lundegårde, the cobblestones play havoc with their footwear. Her mother wobbles off to the road in the mornings. Three kilometres is a long way in a squall, she takes rain bonnets into stock, water-resistant mascara. In the evenings they have stew, one of the burners doesn't work. A smell of wet wool emanates from the walls, the wallpaper lets go, it's green and blue patterned. She copies the pattern into her squared exercise book while sitting at the coffee table. There's a scratching underneath the floorboards, their clothes won't dry. But worst of all is the yard, they wish never again to live with cobblestones or even anything like in the country, her mother walks on flagstones and tarmac, end of.

15

Steffen lives in a villa by the lakes in Maribo. They've got their own jetty, but Steffen advises against swimming in Maribo's lakes just at the moment, there's a risk of allergic reaction to the algae. They stand at the end of the jetty, look out across the water. The trees along the bank are changing colour, a pair of ducks flap. Steffen turns towards her, tugs on the tie of her anorak:

'A cup of coffee would be nice now,' he says.

They go back through the garden, the carport's still empty. In the kitchen he washes his hands and fills the coffee maker with water. There's a bowl with different kinds of fruit in it on the table, plus a jar of vitamin pills.

'Where the hell's she put it?' he says, opening one cupboard then another, eventually finding the coffee. He dispenses four measures meticulously. His hair reaches almost to his shoulders, he has a habit of flicking it away from his face. He turns and smiles at her:

'We can sit here, if that's all right.'

'Here's fine.'

She pulls out a chair and sits down. Opens her bag, produces her pencil case plus a timetable for the Lolland line. There's a demonstration next Wednesday, they're arranging the group travel there and back.

'I'm thinking we can go on the 7.50,' she says, she underlines the departure.

'That's that sorted, then,' he says.

They laugh a bit. He picks up the timetable, studies the front cover. It's a very noiseless coffee maker.

'Have some,' he says, indicating the fruit bowl. She reaches for the vitamin pills, holds the jar up in front of her, they laugh again.

They have a fruit bowl in the living room too, it's on the coffee table. The bananas are brown, because of the sun in the afternoons, says Steffen. In his bedroom there are two Soviet posters on the wall. It's because he has Russian, their study trip's to Moscow. While she views the posters, he rummages in a box, he finds some photos and holds one out for her to look at:

'This was the best thing we saw over there,' he says.

It shows a boy with a crutch and legs that are two different lengths, he's waiting at a crossing. There's also a photo of an elderly man in a wheelchair.

'There are so many myths about the Soviet Union,' he says.

She stares at the photo for some time, she nods repeatedly:

'Yes. Yes,' she says.

Back in the living room they take their clothes off and lie on top of each other on the sofa. Steffen's face smiles down at her, but he doesn't move at all. They lie quite still. She smiles a bit too. Some time passes with them lying there like that. The sun breaks through the cloud and indeed shines directly on the fruit bowl. Now he looks dejected, he pulls himself up into a seated position.

'There's something I need to tell you,' he says.

She sits up too.

'Let's go into the kitchen,' he says.

They get dressed again and go through. He gulps a mouthful of water straight from the tap, wipes his mouth with his sleeve.

'I'm not allowed to go on Wednesday,' he says.

'Oh. That's a shame,' she says.

The fridge kicks in, they both turn and look. It's nearly four o'clock. They go out via the utility room, there's mud on her shoes. Outside in front of the house he shifts his weight from foot to foot on account of the cold air. She waves when she reaches the gate. Swings her bag over her shoulder and starts walking, some leaves descend one at a time, the name of the road is something containing blue.

16

October is long because they're awaiting results from the hospital and because there's so much homework. Practically every day after school she lies on the settee trying to pull herself together. She falls asleep and wakes with arms and legs numb. Realistically she can do most of it on the bus the next morning, especially if it goes via Holeby. So mostly it's a mental thing. In the kitchen she halves an apple, makes herself a sandwich. Leaves the knife on the edge of the sink. Her mother comes home and empties her shopping bag, they're only having yoghurt. There's the recurring discussion about the butter knife, but it's not that big an issue. They sit for a bit in the dim light of the late afternoon, her mother declares she'll change into her comfy clothes. But she can't pull herself together either. They fight then over the local weekly, at last they get to their feet. She makes to run around the dining table, but it's pushed back against the wall now, they move it the day before. Her mother snatches the paper from out of her hands, they laugh and laugh, get their breath back gradually. She sits down with her homework by the radiator. The wind's full on from the east.

The next day it's blowing a gale, she rings the ward discreetly to find out what's what, she pretends to be someone else. It's the afternoon, she's in on her own. The nurse says she'll ring her back. She sits at the table, fortunately the phone doesn't ring. Her mother comes home, they make coffee, switch the lights on too. They gaze through the window, talk about garlands among other things. Her mother says it's time she got started on the dinner and heads into the kitchen. The radio goes on, her mother sings along. Then the telephone rings, it's the nurse, she's Swedish or Norwegian. She speaks clearly, but considerately. She reads aloud from the records. The patient expresses great surprise at the severity of her illness. Her mother bounds into the living room with two potatoes. She finds a telephone conversation taking place and beats a quiet retreat. Now the music changes, again her mother sings along. The doctors can relieve the symptoms, but the condition can't be cured. Her school bag is dumped on the floor, she sits in front of it with her back to the rest of the room. Six months, perhaps a year. The dinner's ready, they can eat now. They eat now.

They clear the table together, she insists on washing up on her own. Her mother lifts both arms above her head, hands the apron over gladly. She dries the plates in front of the open window, the pane rattles.

Afterwards she sits with some maths, her mother lines up liquorice allsorts for her on the coffee table. She manages to express that she's feeling very full and goes to her room. She lies down under the bedspread. It's Indian cotton, predominantly bright purple. She shouts in to say she's asleep.

About painting the living room to match a candlestick. All you have to do is take the candlestick with you wrapped in a tea towel in your bag and show it to the man at the paint shop. He sells doormats and wicker baskets too, but they've enough wicker baskets as it is. One's over by the television with the local weekly in it, another's behind the settee with unheeded knitting. The coffee table is actual mahogany, it rolls. Hairs and fibres catch in its castors. There exists a standard lamp, the light falls on the day's pile of crumbs. The one who takes the last piece washes the tin. Coconut loaf cake diminishes endlessly, treacle tart. The light in the windowsill, the sky above the mother-in-law's tongue.

18

At the bottom of Stationsvej it turns out there's a station. The platform is potholed and overgrown, the tracks hidden under withered grass. Her mother goes the long way round with her shopping bag, she's off work, but the shopping still has to be done. Behind the high street and then a left, out along the footpath after the crossroad, between euonymus and bone-dry elder. Here a fleeting idea about preserves is fostered. By the station building someone calls out to her, but she doesn't know what the time is. She goes back to the high street and in the Co-op buys milk and cheese spread. Then she can't keep herself away from the shop after all. Marna's behind the counter with her filler-in's cloth, her face lights up. They have a cup of coffee in the back room, the conversation revolves around savoury pancakes. Marna knows very well there's a station at the bottom of Stationsvej. Because her husband jogs. Then there are customers, two elderly ladies. They're looking to try some undershirts, it takes place in the back room. Her mother puts her cup in the sink, jabs an apologetic finger at it. Marna smiles and bats a hand. Her mother goes out through the back door, along the footpath in the direction of the fire station. She reminds herself as always to swing her arms, even now with the shopping bag. A person can exercise quite satisfactorily even in a living room. A solemn boy dangles from the fence up ahead, she shakes her head:

'You mustn't do that,' she says as she approaches, he likewise shakes his head, jumps down. He keeps looking at her.

'I live there,' he says.

'Good for you,' she says and is about to carry on, only then he raises his little voice:

'My sister says you're the nicest-looking lady in the whole town.'

'Does she? How very kind. You thank her from me,' she says, headshaking shifting now into nodding on both parts, reaching the beer depot she even turns round and waves. Back in the flat she takes out a notepad, still in her overcoat, she writes: *The days bring new experiences, good ones frequently too*. A bit later she adds *as a rule*, but crosses it out again, she doesn't care for the expression, replaces it with *in general*, inserts *at least*, swaps *frequently* for *often*, moves *often*.

19

The first place they live isn't the first place. It's high up in the Kongeleddet flats. They have hanging plants and the settee is floral-patterned. A birthday is held for her with very few candles. This is while there are male cousins. Her mother delivers her every morning into a friendly environment with boiled herring, great care is taken regarding the bones. They talk about the day on the bicycle home, every event is sung. Her mother sells milk and eggs and soap. When summer comes they'll stand on their tiptoes in crochet dresses, long after this cold frost. They wheel the bicycle into the basement, carry up the things, sit in the living room in their own two worlds. They have a wall sconce, but not a rocking chair, a rocking chair is for old people, and they're not old.

20

Bob's having a party, they bike to Gerringe on Tove's bike. Tove pedals, the road is long and straight. She sits on the luggage rack with a torch Tove's dad attaches earlier with string. They undo the knots when they get round the corner so she can hop on. Her hair is tied in two impossible plaits. The bike wobbles, Tove's got sheepskin mittens on. It's a mild and quiet evening. She endeavours to make her self light, sits with legs aloft.

'I'll have to get mine fixed,' she says.

'Yes, this one's got no gears,' Tove says.

They take a break by the side of the main road. Tove wants to smoke, they lean the bike against a signpost. She herself stands with the torch between two fingers like a cigarette. She shines the beam into the fields.

'Look! Nothing!' Tove says, and they laugh, the bike nearly falls over. They drink a few beers as well before leaving the house. Balances are regained, they press on, now wheeling. It's Tove's suggestion:

'Let's just wheel it the rest of the way,' she says with smoke on her voice, and she nods her reply into the darkness with the torch:

'Okey-dokey.'

Bob lives on a proper farm, it's something they're not anticipating. Tove's there last summer, admittedly, but that's an after-party. His parents grow beet, they've got livestock too. They're told so by his younger brother soon after they enter the yard. People are everywhere inside the house with bottles of beer, someone's making spaghetti and a creamy sauce. It's the girl they call the ethnologist. Tove sits down on a pile of coats in the passage along with a few from her class. They sit with cigarettes held high, she stands a while and smiles beside them, moves on into the dining room, finds the bar. The money's to be put in an ovenproof dish. She buys a beer, Bob steps out of an embrace over by the window, lifts two fingers in acknowledgement. She lifts likewise, goes through into the next room with her beer. Music's playing, she doesn't know what. She taps her thigh with her free hand as she goes. The sauce is still being stirred in the kitchen, more milk is added. The ethnologist is wearing jeans, she turns round smiling with the wooden spoon. At the table they're debating, something about the county council. The sauce catches on the pan, shrieks and laughter, back in the passage they're still immersed in talk on top of the coats. She veers halfway into a crowded bedroom, recognises the back of Steffen's head, spins round and carries on into a utility room. The washing machine is running a cycle. There's a steep wooden staircase with a door at the top, she goes up the stairs and through into a cold loft with exposed roofing sheets. Light escapes from a room at the far end. She walks over and opens the door a crack, a man and a woman sit inclined over a coffee table eating smørrebrød, it's Bob's parents.

'Enter, enter, don't be shy,' Bob's mum says.

'Enjoy,' she says, and is rooted to the spot, but Bob's dad waves her in with his fork:

'Come in and shut the door!'

They're watching German television, a music programme.

'He's a proper rascal that one,' Bob's mum says with a laugh, and lifts a lettuce leaf.

They offer her a piece with roast beef. She smiles and declines, takes a swig of her beer. Then footsteps sound on the floor of the loft, it's Bob's younger brother:

'Uh, the pane's broken in the passage door again,' he says.

'Is anyone hurt?' Bob's mum says.

'Are you coming or going?' says Bob's dad.

'I'll tape it up, there's no panic,' Bob's brother says, she seizes the chance to beat a retreat, lifts her beer in parting.

'What's happened?' she enquires of Bob's brother as they cross back through the loft.

'Oh, just people knocking too hard, it happens every other day,' he says.

She helps Bob's younger brother sweep up the shards, she inspects the entire floor, including under all the shoes and boots. Even after he's finished taping up and goes off to see to a cow that keeps bellowing, she continues. There's no longer a shard in sight, but she does find a packet of cigarettes in a wellington boot. She puts it on top of the drawers, then the passage door opens, it's Hafni in a long sweater, her cheeks are flushed:

'Hey, you've plaited your hair! Do you smoke?'

She's not staying, her brother's picking her up shortly. They've got visitors at home, plus the fact of a maths exercise to hand in on Monday. She's wearing an off-the-shoulder top under her sweater, she finds them a pair of woolly socks each in the drawers:

'This floor is so cold. Is it fun?'

'I got to see the loft.'

'OK! Can you buy wine?'

'Beer.'

'Ugh. I'll have to smoke then, can I have one?'

They wander through the house in their woolly socks, Hafni with her cigarette. In the kitchen she asks a boy to hold it while she gets a glass of water. She drinks it all at once, afterwards beams a big smile. They resume their wander, people tread on their socks. In the living room they embark on a dance, but then Hafni gets talking to someone from Darket. They speak ardently into each other's ears in front of the corner unit.

She buys another beer and goes into the kitchen again. As she stands drinking, Steffen comes into the room. She stays where she is with the bottle poised in front of her mouth, until he comes up to her. He places a hand on her back. A girl with long, dark hair goes past and says:

'Aw, you're cute together.'

But then fortunately Bob appears in the doorway holding a guitar in the air, everyone shouts for Steffen to play.

She sits freezing in the yard with beer number three. She can't really feel the effect. The guitar strums from the living room, in the byre the cow bellows still. The bathroom window opens, Bob pokes his head out and cries:

'Be near me!'

She smiles at him and lifts the two fingers it seems she's started lifting too. The window closes. She gets up and goes inside into the hall, searches for the torch, finds it in the pocket of Tove's coat. Outside again she makes away down the long approach. White mist shimmers in the beam, a raw smell of clay soil ploughed. Nearing the main road she pauses. She needs to think, she can't work out if it's better going home over the fields.

'Narh,' she says, and sways on her feet, perhaps she is a bit tipsy after all, but then Hafni comes charging along the rutted track from behind:

'Is it you, do you want a lift?'

'Where are you going?'

'We've got visitors, I told you. Torsten's coming at half past, he'll be here in a minute.'

'It's the wrong way.'

'It doesn't matter. He can turn round at the top.'

'No, I mean wrong for where I live.'

'Ah! That doesn't matter either.'

For this reason Torsten drives her home and it turns out not to be out of his way, Torsten's friend who's in the car needs dropping off in Fuglse. She understands they've come from another friend's and that they work together on the ferries. All three are on a gap year. Hafni sits behind her brother, she leans forward and slaps him on the shoulder.

'Are you drunk?' he says.

'No!' says Hafni, the friend twists round, switches the little cabin light on and scrutinises them both:

'They look all right to me,' he says, and switches it off again.

They drop her off on the square. Before she locates the handle in the car door, the friend jumps out and opens it for her. She sees that he's wearing white shoes and is rather short.

'Sleep well,' he says.

'Night night!' Hafni shouts, and a moment later someone says:

'Here!'

A hand reaches out with the torch, the car pulls away. She illuminates the sixty metres home, the pavement in front of her feet, shines the beam across the street, into the foil of Favør's blanked-out windows.

It's her mother and Marna and the odd-job man who refurbish the shop seven years ago. They do it over a weekend, morning to night. They assemble stands and racks, the odd-job man undertakes the shelving and the lighting. In the middle of everything they change their minds and flip the furnishings round. The dressing gowns go best away from the counter. But they can't put the stock out until last thing tomorrow, there's a long way to go yet. They toil until their hair's wet, they laugh a lot in the process. Marna calls a break now and then. She's brought boiled eggs with her, only not quite boiled enough. So they keep themselves going on coffee and brambles from the yard. The local weekly looks in and promises to come back for the opening, her mother tells her so when they sit for a minute on a garden chair out the back:

'Do you know what, the paper's coming to take some pictures on Tuesday.'

'Are you going to be in the paper, Mum?'

'Yes, but not until next week.'

'So not the next one but the next after that?'

'Yes. If they're any good, that is.'

'I can't wait,' she says, her mother widens her eyes and nods, there are four eggs on top of a cardboard box next to them, the odd-job man's cigarette smoulders in the ashtray.

'We're starving hungry, can you pop home and make us something?' her mother says.

'What can I make?'

'Whatever you like. It's up to you. Just bring it over when you're ready.'

'I will,' she says, and makes haste to Nørregade.

They've a carrier bag full of loose recipes, plus a cookbook. But they've also the old women's weeklies in the suitcase, she peruses them first. She contemplates beefburgers and a bright green cake by the name of *savarin*. She places the magazines she's looked at in the suitcase lid. There are three so far. Now she determines to be thorough and studies the cookbook from the beginning, starters and all. You can make fried eggs out of pineapple, if you've peaches and cheese. But perhaps they've had it with eggs for today. She dwells on canapés and nibbles, having toothpicks on hand, but then there's the problem of carrying. She sits on the floor in the kitchen, she's got a big midge bite on her ankle. It keeps itching, so she gets to her feet for the cloth. She wrings it in cold water and presses it against the bite, the water dribbles down her foot. There's a clam gratin as well. They have one last summer at the fashion show at Bang's, with garlic and a crispy crust. On the back of a soufflé recipe her mother's written *condensed milk, wash skirting boards down*. She remembers the day well. She comes home from school, all the windows are open, warm air is streaming in. The living room smells of hay. Her mother goes about with a scarf on her head, they're having guests, the table's already set. They make eight in all including her, but she's allowed to stay in her room if she prefers. She has a bowlful of crisps all to herself, after she's greeted the guests. In the other room they laugh, cutlery and glasses chink. Her mother laughs on as she fetches the gravy, shortly afterwards they're silent a moment while raising their glasses. But the laughter quickly returns. They each tell a story about making a fool of themselves, her mother once trips on her flares. Later they talk about an anniversary the others are going to tomorrow. There are dessert chocolates to go with the coffee, her mother arranges them on a plate. They stand at the window and wave when the guests leave two by two. In the morning she wakes to her mother's crying, she gets up to see what's the matter, but she isn't crying, and it isn't morning either. She decides at last on cheese sandwiches. If they've any jam, she'll put jam on some. She's rather hungry herself now, she takes an apple and cuts it into pieces. She puts the pieces in a saucepan, adds some water and stews them. After that she presses the stewed apple pieces with peel and pips and core through a sieve, the mash oozes down into the bowl. She sprinkles on some sugar and eats while sitting on the worktop. The sieve is hard to clean, it's rusty as it is. She keeps squirting it with washing-up liquid, can soon barely see for suds, she must let the water run and run. Then she discovers they've hardly any cheese left, but it's not a problem. She can do some with jam and some with cheese. The cheese has a thick rind to it and covering the rind there's the wax her mother eats by mistake. She cuts away both rind and wax with the bread knife, a very small cube is all that remains. She switches the radio on and turns the dial, a song comes on that she likes. She feels an urge to write down the lyrics and learn them off by heart, she finds the biro in the drawer along with some greaseproof, but the greaseproof tears when she tries to write on it. She goes into the living room for some proper paper, and from the living room into the hall, and from the hall back into the kitchen, and into the living room again.

22

Scattered snowflakes hang in the air, Palle steps out of Clothes Man with a brush. He sets about sweeping something up, stops and looks at the sky, sweeps on. Her mother's on the step in front of the shop, she looks up too. She herself comes wheeling her bike from the bicycle shop, the odd snowflake touches her face. Palle raises his brush, her mother spreads out her arms. Then she's got customers, a dog is parked.

She crosses the street with her bike, Palle waves her over.

'Just look at my little Ficus,' he says, they look down on a pile of shards and potting soil, two small broken twigs. Some snowflakes have settled on his jumper, it's light blue with a brown stripe across the chest. He's tall and slim, his trousers are with turn-ups. Ever the mannequin, he always says, now the dog begins to yap, it's a Samoyed, its front quarters are halfway up the step.

'That's a shame.'

'I only just paid forty for it.'

'With the pot?'

'No chance. You pipe down,' he says, they both turn their heads to the dog, its back end shudders with every yap, then fortunately the door opens, transaction complete.

Her mother's behind the counter in her cobalt-blue set, both hands flat on the glass top. She reaches to her rear for the Fidji, two squirts at the ceiling.

'Did you get it mended?' she says, her bracelets tinkle.

'It was closed.'

'Tsk. You'll have to try again another day. Do you want some tea?'

'Have you started drinking tea?'

'Not really. Only it's snowing now.'

The tea tastes of coffee, the water's from the coffee maker.

'There's an aftertaste. Perhaps it's Fidji,' her mother says.

They sit on the stools in the back room, stare through the shop at the street. The dusk is descending, a thin layer of snow stands out white on the Co-op's canopy.

'I feel sorry for Palle,' she says.

'Yes, he was as chuffed as could be,' says her mother.

They lift their mugs, sip synchronous mouthfuls.

'Ugh,' says her mother.

They laugh a bit. Her mother digs at her gently with the toe of her shoe, the shoes are the ones they call Christian the Fourths. She leans forward on her stool:

'Here's Havnegade. No. They're going past.'

There's an hour and a half until closing. They decide to have beer porridge tonight, they've got the sweet malt beer, eggs too in fact.

'I'll make it,' her mother says and points a finger into the air, ting-a-ling, it's Havnegade after all, they're looking to buy nighties.

At home in the flat she stands at the window reading English for tomorrow. The cars glide along the high street, the man from the paint shop struggles with a sign. She has trouble with the word *colonel*, she says it out loud to herself a number of times. A man waits to cross over, he's wearing his hood up, the hood follows the movements of his head. Then at last it's safe to cross, he scurries towards the phone box. The snow descends in the glow of the street lamps, when the street lamps come on, when it snows.

23

Hafni's brother's friend phones and invites her out to Restaurant Lysemose. She pulls the receiver all the way round the back of the settee, her mother's gone to bed a while ago.

'A good steak,' he says.

'I can't,' she says. 'Just a minute.'

She puts the receiver down and goes to the kitchen. Opens a cupboard, closes it again. Then goes back.

'I can go for a stroll,' she says.

'A walk, you mean?'

'Yes.'

'When would suit?'

'Sunday, perhaps.'

'That's fine, I should have the car then too,' he says.

Her mother calls for her, she's lying with a duvet rolled up behind her head.

'Who was it?' she says.

'Were you asleep?'

'Not really.'

'Can't you sleep?'

'Of course I can, give over,' her mother says, props herself on her elbow:

'Do you know, I'd quite like to go with you to Maribo one day.'

'What for?'

'Just to see something different. A look round the centre, take in the square.'

'There's not much in the square.'

'There must be a bench at least?'

'All right. We'll do that, Mum,' she says and fetches a glass of water, puts it on the bedside table.

Sunday afternoon he gets out of the car on Mellemtorvet, a white shoe appears first. He looks left then right then left again, crosses the empty street. She ducks down quickly onto the settee, jumps up as quickly again when he rings the bell, she manages to stand alternately in the doorway and on the landing, then he appears:

'Hi.'

'Yes, hi.'

He's wearing a bomber jacket, he pats a pocket.

'Are you in the car?' she says.

'Just about.'

They both laugh, then step inside into the hall.

'You can hang it there,' she says, and indicates where.

As he searches for the loop, her mother emerges from the bedroom:

'Oh, hello!'

'This is Kasper Hjort, and this is my mum,' she says.

They shake hands, he's still clutching his bomber jacket.

'What a nice day,' her mother says.

'Brilliant,' he says, and a moment later when once again they're on their own in the hall:

'My dad was going to use it. Only he took my mum's instead.'

She nods, he keeps his shoes on.

'Car,' he says.

*

They stand at the window in her room. She points out a chimney stack, he tilts his head. The weather is very fine for November, the poplars by the playing fields sway gently against the blue sky. She leans forward, his hand settles on her shoulder. He plays football, he's been playing ten years, the hairs of his armpit are slightly sticky. Now they lie on the floor next to the bed, his smell brings to mind boxwood, it's very pleasant. He's thirsty, so she goes to the kitchen for something to drink. She finds a note on the worktop, *Getting some air wth Palle. There's biscuits*, but she settles for water and apple. They've the flat to themselves for several hours. At one point they sit with no clothes on at the dining table, he's genuinely impressed by the view and how big the lawns are in front of the local authority buildings.

He's on nights tonight, he needs to go home and rest. There's a whole group from their year on the ferries, they have a good laugh with each other. He and Torsten take turns to drive, the others chip in for the petrol. She goes downstairs into the street with him in her shirt, the air is icy cold. They chat for a bit, kiss the once before he gets in.

'Do you always wear them?' he says with a nod at her shoes.

'No,' she says.

'Well, look after yourself,' he says, and kisses her again, this time on her hand, which she presents through the open car door.

'I liked his jacket, it's rather smart,' her mother says as they sit down at the table that evening. They're having a stew from yesterday, her mother eats with appetite, serves herself more rice.

'Yes,' she says, she keeps thinking about his unclothed crotch at the table only a short time before.

'A nice head of dark hair he has too,' her mother says.

'He's a quarter Chinese.'

'Is he really? I'm not keen on you driving about in that car, though.'

'It's not his own.'

'Well, thank goodness for that. I feel better about it now.'

'I'm actually not that interested, Mum.'

'In the car?'

'No.'

'Oh,' her mother says, her cutlery poised a second: 'That's a shame.'

Before going to bed she swaps her posters round. She dispenses with one, the dove of peace. She rolls it up and puts it at the back of the wardrobe, under the rail. While she's there, she goes through her clothes. She no longer intends to wear dungarees. She experiments with a high ponytail, packs her bag. In the kitchen she prepares her sandwiches, four pieces of crisp-bread with cheese and chives. She changes her mind about the cheese and eats it, her mother appears in her nightie, observes the now bereft crispbread:

'That's not food.'

'Sort of it is.'

They hear at once that hail then falls, the hailstones even batter the window. They stand and look out, until they're cold.

24

One Monday in the long break she buckles her bag and puts on her coat, she goes round the back of the centre to the station and gets on the Nykøbing train. She knows it's a Monday because they've got music in the morning and the music teacher sits at the snare drum and whispers through his teeth, *till Tuesday, till Tuesday*, then slips instead into *till tomorrow* and everyone groans. From the train she looks out on black fields, teetering tractor loads on grit roads. The beet campaign's still on. The sweet, mushy smell hangs in Nykøbing's streets, she carries her bag over one arm, then the other. Up in the town centre, many of the shops have Christmas displays in their windows, she stops in front of the ironmonger's and looks at a flock of reindeer. A woman in a Loden coat comes to a halt beside her:

'What a smart bag that is. Have a good day,' she says before swinging into the shop.

There are sprigs of spruce in the planters outside Kvickly. She takes a basket, wanders among the bread shelves. Moves on to the soaps, examines all the lotions and creams, she's looking for a Christmas present, something they don't stock in the shop. She plumps for a shower gel and natural fibre bath mitten set, but changes her mind, pivots on her heel and returns the box to the shelf. Leaves the empty basket on the floor, then thinks better of it and goes back, picks it up and takes it with her and drops it into the stack. On her way through the checkout she holds up her hands, the checkout woman smiles:

'Right-o,' she says.

She goes over to what must be the abbey church, and through into some gardens. There are many kinds of withered herbs in the beds, greys and grey-greens, with curled-up little leaves full of other bigger leaves. She's thirsty. Back in the high street she sits briefly on a bench, but it's far too cold, she goes up to the square and into a clothes shop to get warm, tries a single sweater on. She pores a while through a pile of scarves, decides on a pink one and has it nicely gift-wrapped and put in a bag. She wanders down towards the harbour. Passes a pub with snow-decorated windows, a man inside raises his beer and gives her a nod. She walks along the quayside and looks out across the water, wonders if anyone's watching her. She thinks more about that than about the way the water shimmers in the dull grey light. But then someone actually waves their arms at her from over by a pile of gravel, a forklift comes tearing along, it's a work zone. She angles quickly away between two sheds and returns to the road, follows it along the fjord.

Her shoulders ache and she's very thirsty. She believes there's a baker's shop somewhere behind some big villas, she determines to find it and buy a carton of chocolate milk. But she'll go a bit further past the red housing blocks first. An elderly man grapples with a Christmas tree on a ground-floor balcony, she transfers her bag again onto her other arm. Now she comes upon a sign saying *Ergotherapy, X-ray*. She turns into the hospital grounds, follows sluggishly the narrow paths between the buildings. A patient with tubes stands breathing by a bush, nods:

'It's just over there.'

Then she's at the main entrance. She goes through the revolving door, avoids immediately some dark stains on the floor. But they may easily be coffee. Inside, a milling about of dressing gowns, socks pulled up over chalk-white legs, but visitors too, in bright-coloured winter coats. She makes a beeline for the hospital kiosk, she can just as well buy something to drink here. But as she stands and considers the soft drinks, a towelling-clad arm reaches in front of her and grasps a lemonade, she steps back and unwittingly detaches thereby a shelf tag that drops to the floor. And while she's crouching down to pick it up, she notices that everyone around her is wearing slippers. Perhaps the kiosk is reserved for patients. She retreats hastily to the foyer, one more time around the stains, but now the revolving door is blocked by an illogical stretcher and queuing has commenced at the side entrance. It occurs to her that there must be a toilet in the vicinity and thereby a tap, sure enough there's a sign away to her left. But when she goes inside she finds it's a very unpleasant toilet. She leaves it and ventures round a corner. Along the corridor she comes to a small waiting area with four vacant chairs, there's a table too and some tired weeklies. A jug of blackcurrant squash moreover and a stack of plastic cups. She puts her bag down on the floor. Approaches the table. The automatic door opens and a nurse comes clomping through:

'Can I help you?' she says with a smile, in Swedish or Norwegian.

She shakes her head, picks up her bag and turns back, fortunately the revolving door allows free passage once more.

*

She's wandered off course. The sky is dense and grey, the smell of beet still pungent, although she must be near the outskirts now. She waits at a busy road, watches some jackdaws on the ridge of a roof. They're in motion all the time. When one lands, another takes off. At last a car stops, the driver waves her across.

On the other side of the road she follows the line of a hedge. Behind it there turns out to be a cemetery, a man chugs around with a trailerload of spruce. She spots a tap with the stub of a rubber hose attached, goes in through a gate, the fine gravel leaves white marks on her shoes. Reaching the tap she stands a moment and looks around, turns it on and bends down. But she loses her nerve and settles for a quick wash of her hands, the water's freezing cold. She cuts across a lawn and goes back out through the gate, continues through a sizeable residential area comprising sedate villas, past rows of yellow housing blocks, and then lo and behold the baker's is there on the corner. But they're closed today, a solitary creamless cake has been left in the window. There's nothing for it but to follow the road back towards town. After the park she branches off and crosses a parking area to the rear of Kvickly. There's no one at the sausage stand. The woman inside clatters a container, leans out across the counter:

'Do you want a free sausage?'

'Me?'

'Yes, it'll only be thrown out,' she says and extends the sausage towards her with a pair of tongs, followed by a bread roll wrapped in a serviette.

'How do,' says a passing man and smiles at them both, she smiles back and continues on her way with sausage and bread, past Kvickly and down into

Jernbanegade. She can't eat until she's had something to drink. But she can't go in and buy something either with a sausage in her hand. She doesn't even know if she can actually eat the sausage. She places it cautiously in a bin at the end of the street, covers it up with the serviette. The bread she takes with her. On the platform she discovers she's lost the bag with the scarf in it. She thinks back through the afternoon, looks up at the sugar factory's two white pillars of steam.

25

Tove Dunk eats what must be sixteen puff dumplings in a Danish lesson, for which reason they're now flat out on separate benches in the school gym. Their shoes and bags are strewn haphazardly outside the changing-room door. It's breaktime, voices are heard from the yard.

'Are you going out with Kasper Hjort?' says Tove.

'Not exactly.'

'You do know he's a conservative?'

'His mum's a social worker.'

'Oh, OK,' Tove says, she slides herself backwards and forwards with a socked foot on the wooden floor. They're meant to clean up after themselves until further notice following PE, they take turns to push a wet mop around. The mop is wrung in a bucket in the storage room, no one can be bothered to change the water.

'Yuck,' Tove says, they're standing staring now into the bucket, a grey scum containing soggy fluff rests on the surface. They're on their way to the small library in a minute, there are newspapers and journals there, Tove's intending to copy out a poem for one thing. They nudge the bucket with their feet, the scum shudders. The mop is laid across a stand with the yarn flopped over the edge. They hear someone's footfall, it's one of the PE teachers.

'What are you doing here?' she says.

'We're washing the floor,' says Tove.

They go over and gather up their shoes and bags,

change back into their clothes in the changing room. Tove finds an unsmoked cigarette in the windowsill. The air is mild, it's raining gently. Under the pent roof, Tove gets a light from her German teacher. She blows the smoke in different directions:

'It's the maddest of days,' she says.

In the side building, the door of the small library is locked. Tove says they can go the back way through a classroom, so they walk on down the corridor. Outside the classroom in question a boy stands leaning against the wall, Tove exchanges a few words with him before they go in.

Fortunately, the back door of the small library is open, and there's no one inside. They find the journal on a dusty shelf and sit down at the desk. Tove starts reading, it's quite some time before she turns the page.

'You could read your own,' she says without looking up.

Someone's left a plate of seasonal ginger snaps on a corner of the desk. A bite has been taken from one. She finds a different issue of the same journal on the shelf, it has a woman wearing dark lipstick on the front cover. She tries to read slowly, the poems are very short. The bell rings falteringly for the next lesson. They don't get up, Tove has a free period now anyway. Teaching commences in the classroom next door. A student conducts a presentation in a low, unwavering tone, the words are indistinguishable through the double door. After a while a key is inserted into the library door proper, it's her religious studies teacher sporting a fisherman's smock.

'Oh, you look like you've made yourselves comfortable,' she says with a smile, and they nod back and smile too.

The religious studies teacher searches a shelf with her head tipped to one side.

'Care for a seasonal ginger snap?' Tove says.

'Yes, please,' the religious studies teacher says, and takes one. She consumes it almost soundlessly, sucks it soggy. They sit with their heads in their separate issues. Eventually the religious studies teacher gives up her search and leaves the room. They share the rest of the ginger snaps between them, apart from the one that's missing a bite. That one they throw out of the window, into the herbaceous border below.

26

Her mother has the flat to herself and tidies up in a cardboard box. It's the particularly sturdy cardboard box from previous times. Double-bottomed and double-sided. It's not so big that it won't go on the top shelf of the wardrobe along with the tartan suitcase. She stands on a chair and pulls it out, lugs it over onto the bed. Sits down beside it and gets her breath back. From here she can see the tall birch tree in the yard behind Favør, and a wall and some corrugated iron. She's distinctly satisfied with her hands. The bedspread bunches, she smooths it, she's actually only forty-one. She can wear almost any type of heel. A hood dryer is switched on beneath her, bottles chink at the depot. The sky is a pasty white, the air almost certainly dank and cold. She sits up straight, a palm at rest on each trouser leg.

27

'You're quiet of late. Is it because of Kasper Hjort?' Hafni says.

They're sitting in the centre pub with two cups of tea, the holiday starts an hour ago. They share a portion of frites too, they draw patterns in the dip, laugh a bit. An elderly man at the next table leans over a plate of among other things peas.

It's the second time she sits in the centre pub. The first time's with Tove Dunk and the rest of them last week, she arrives after everyone else, the others are drinking a dark kind of ale. She goes up to the bar, points back at their table and says:

'One of them.'

The barman doesn't get what she means. He shakes his head, smacks his brow. Bob looks up, rises to his feet then and comes to her rescue. He orders a big glass of the same dark ale for her:

'Anything for the lady,' he says. They go back to the table together. Two carrier bags of Christmas presents sag under Bob's chair, most are for his younger brother, soldering irons and ear protection. His parents are getting dessert dishes, but he doesn't buy them until the last minute. Tove and Steffen and someone called Henrik Strøm are going to Travemünde on Christmas Eve. They're catching the ferry mid-afternoon, taking cheese and biscuits with them. It's to escape the madness, instead of Christmas presents they get money for the trip. Tove intends too to bring some grapes and perhaps a homemade rugbrød, red wine they'll buy in the duty free. But it's not about drinking, they just want the breathing space. To sit on the deck and look at the sea. Tove lights a long cigarette, it's from her advent calendar. She blows the smoke obliquely upwards, into the lampshade. It swirls between their faces.

Hafni's spending Christmas at her mother's sister's in Kalvehave, they'll be sixteen at the minimum. She counts them on her fingers. They'll have grab-and-go hot dogs, then walk to church, and afterwards there's goose. They'll be sleeping on air mattresses around the house amid the smell of spruce. Hafni's as excited as a child. The only minus is the unexpected physics report to be handed in just after the holiday, but it's the same rotten deal for all. They agree to phone each other between Christmas and New Year, neither of them has plotted the results into the table.

They walk to the station together, wave to each other from their separate buses. All the way home she looks out at the fields, the fat, loamy furrows. It rains, the holiday lasts twelve days. Her mother's getting a bamboo birdcage, and a glasses case.

'You'll never guess what you're getting, Mum,' she says later that same afternoon, her mother widens her eyes and beams, throws up her hands. On Christmas Eve they sit for some time while staring at the birdcage, they open and close its door. Eventually they come up with putting a fern in it, they rearrange the entire room on account of this new element, it's like the time with the glass trolls, it becomes a completely different home.

28

Steffen and Kasper Hjort have an altercation outside Mona Lisa the day after Christmas, Steffen's walking home from his paternal grandparents'. It's because Kasper says something disparaging about Steffen's hair as he goes past. Kasper's drunk and has stepped out onto the pavement to get some fresh air, he's struggling with a few things at the moment, apparently he feels a need to assert himself. Steffen wheels round and bloodies Kasper's nose. They're both a bit shocked afterwards, they end up sitting in an outhouse talking for over two hours, now they might be going to play badminton together.

She hears about it from Hafni's brother in the Co-op the day before New Year's Eve, he's standing at one of the chillers with a long joint of meat. He and some others are going to Fejø to celebrate. It fazes her bumping into him in the Co-op, but he's come straight from the ferries. Besides, their meat's very good. He asks what her own plans are, she's going to a party at Tove Dunk's with four others, they're having ham and creamed kale, but she doesn't tell him that. Hafni's brother puts the meat into his basket and puts the basket down on the floor. He proceeds to relate an episode involving two Swedes that same morning. He looks at her very directly, it prompts her to handle some items in the chiller. The Swedes get their kroner and Deutschmarks mixed up, but she doesn't quite catch the rest. The strip lighting above him glares down on the crown of his head. His voice is deep and warm, he's thinking of applying for medical school. Now comes her mother, advancing from the bread section with her trolley. She's in her long overcoat, she's draped her scarf over one shoulder. Her small, smiling face turns deliberately from side to side. Hafni's brother glances over his shoulder before he continues. He's concerned as to whether Hafni can get through a possible chemistry exam. What with the time she spends on those horses. Their dad's turning fifty not long after New Year, they're giving him a granite stone engraved with the name of the farm. Her mother sees them, wiggles her fingers in a wave, turns then to closely scrutinise the jam shelves. A moment later though she appears on the other side of the chiller:

'Don't mind me,' she says and picks up a packet of mince, studies it, puts it back, picks up another, puts that one back too. At last she moves on. Hafni's brother gives his nose a good blow. She exploits the moment to wish him a happy new year, it takes a while before he's ready to answer:

'Same to you.'

At the same time, her mother calls to her from the delicatessen:

'Do you want cheese rinds?'

'Have a nice time,' she's able to say, then hurries away.

It's she who puts their items onto the conveyor, her mother stands at the end and packs them into two bags, presents in the process her purse:

'This'll be a fortune,' she says, the checkout lady looks wearily past them at the manager walking by.

They come out into the street and set off briskly

with a bag each, Marna waves from the shop. But they only reach the paint shop before her mother needs a rest, she puts her bag down on the pavement:

'It's digging in, that's all,' she says, and examines her palm, her scarf falls down over her chest. Tossing it back over her shoulder, she gets a tassel in her mouth, she flaps her hand in front of her:

'Argh.'

'Do you want me to carry it?'

'No!' her mother says, and picks up the bag, they walk on side by side and cross over further along.

But when they get home her mother lies down on the settee with her coat on, she stands in the kitchen unbagging the shopping, glances occasionally into the living room through the crack in the door. Her mother lies with her hands on top of her coat, the coat rises and falls. They've bought flour and apples, she puts the apples in the windowsill and tips the flour into the jar, spills a bit, sweeps it up. She folds the two shopping bags together and puts them back where they belong, runs some water into a saucepan, but changes her mind and gets the coffee maker ready with seven measures of coffee. It can always wait until morning. Her mother then clears her throat, she tiptoes in to see to her:

'Do you want some coffee?'

'Were we having coffee, pet?'

'It just needs switching on.'

'There's those biscuits as well.'

'Are you feeling better?'

'I'm all right,' her mother says, tucks a cushion into place at the small of her back.

*

Later, when the coffee's been drunk, they lie down at each end of the settee with the biscuit bowl. Her mother's still got her coat on, they laugh about some crumbs on the collar. Her mother prods her stockinged toe into her side, she nearly drops the bowl. They laugh and laugh. It's getting dark, the garlands rustle outside under the window.

29

This Henrik Strøm invites people round for a party one Saturday night in Rødbyhavn, he lives in Laredo. The temperature's well below freezing, the forecast for the weekend says snow. On the Friday morning her hair, just washed, freezes to ice on her way to the bus. She sits beside Tove, they stare out at nothing the whole thirteen kilometres. Henrik Strøm's going to make pierogi, Tove asks her if she's tried pierogi. Tove's in the dumps about how dark January is, she's looking forward to snow, and even more to spring. At the party they're to drink vodka from little beakers made of wood.

Saturday afternoon she tries on all her clothes before going over to Tove's. They're intending to hang out a few hours then go to Laredo together, Tove's dad's driving them, if he's back. But both he and Tove's mum get stranded in Kerteminde where it's already snowing. Tove's in the kitchen scraping egg off a frying pan. They go to sit in the living room, but the living room smells strongly of smoke after Tove tries to light the fire earlier on. So they return to the kitchen, sit down at the table. Tove's angry with her ex-boyfriend, he speaks disparingingly for example about female guitarists. At the same time, she's having trouble getting over him, he keeps haunting. They think up a name for him, they write it down on a piece of paper. Then Tove crumples it up and puts it in the grate, under a sooty log.

Now it starts snowing, Tove performs a jig. They've plenty of time before the party, so they concoct a drink with tomato juice, she spills a drop on her sweater. But it doesn't matter, she can pick the stain out later. Tove tries on some of her mother's tops, an old cloak too, which they laugh about. They eat some white bread and make themselves another drink, this time with ordinary orange juice, and Tove rolls twenty cigarettes.

They're catching the bus from the dairy, they wrap up with extra scarves around necks and heads. The snow falls thickly, piles against fences and walls. They walk along the road with wine in a carrier bag, they can hardly hear each other on account of their scarves. Down at the dairy they stand under a canopy, they plan to hurry across the road as soon as the bus comes. They wait for some time, and the bus doesn't come. Neither of them's wearing a watch, so they look in through a window and see that it's nearly seven. Tove falls over some low-placed garden lighting.

They decide to walk it. It's only three kilometres and the snow lights everything up, but out on Anden Tværvej they begin to lose heart. They stop just after the road sign, shout to make themselves heard. Snow whips across the road, the easterly wind blows brisk in the open land. Then Tove thumps her on the shoulder and points, it's the bus on its way from town. They stand back into a drift, each with a raised, outstretched arm, Tove even puts the carrier bag down and raises her other arm too. But the bus flies past, they can hardly believe it. The red rear lights speed away along Havnevej. Tove stands quite without expression, still with her arms in the air. A gust of wind blusters across the fields.

30

Her mother's taken into hospital, a Wednesday while she's at school. Palle gives her the news, he's waiting in a duffle coat when she gets off the bus that afternoon. They walk home to the flat together to allow her to dump her bag, she needs something to drink as well. There's no hurry, visiting time lasts until the evening meal. She drinks a glass of water, they leave the kitchen light on. They walk up the high street and into Clothes Man, through the back room and out into the little car park. There they get into a car Palle borrows from his boss. Palle turns the key, but then he feels hot and opens his duffle coat before they set off. They pull out of the car park and pass gently through the town in the direction of the motorway. Palle keeps flexing his hands on the steering wheel, it's the first time he's driving in quite a while.

'It's ten years I should think since the last time,' he says, then indicates the glove compartment with a nod. She looks inside, it contains several bags of liquorice. The fields are still white wherever she looks, but the road is good and black. The wind buffets the car as they turn down the slip road.

'I'm not one for the motorway,' Palle says, fortunately there isn't much traffic, they've hit the lull between ferries. They drive a while without speaking. As they pass Våbensted the low-hanging sun hits the rear-view mirror, he reaches up to adjust it. By now they're driving rather close behind a trailer loaded with upside-down dining chairs. After flexing his hands a couple of times, Palle indicates and pulls out to overtake, the engine roars, but then they're back in the slow lane, the noise returns to normal.

Her mother's head looks very small on the pillow. She props herself up the moment she sees them in the doorway:

'Now there's a welcome sight,' she says with a smile, her cheeks are round and red. A strand of hair hangs down in front of her eye:

'Would you look at me,' she says and blows it away, reaches out to them both, after which she picks up a hairpin from the bedside cabinet.

Palle puts his duffle coat down at the foot end. They sit on either side of her, she on the edge of the bed. Her mother smooths the back of her hand, her hand is warm and dry.

'Do you want a peppermint?' she says.

'No, you keep them,' says Palle.

A forceful cough builds and erupts behind a curtain, her mother lifts her eyebrows. In a pause between two phlegmy expulsions her mother puts a finger to her lips and whispers:

'She's a pain in the neck.'

Then, immediately, in clearer voice:

'So, would you like some coffee?'

'Do they do coffee?' Palle says, her mother nods:

'I'm sure they do.'

Palle goes off in search of coffee and perhaps a biscuit. Combining efforts, they manage to raise the head end while he's gone, her mother winces.

'Are you in pain, Mum?' she says.

'No, but I was, I can tell you. It's a lot better now, though,' her mother says, and smiles, places her hand again on the back of hers.

'Good,' she says, and starts to cry, the tears drip down onto their hands.

'Were you frightened?' her mother says.

'No,' she says, and shakes her head, a tear is slung a short way across the duvet. The door then opens, but it isn't Palle. It's a fair-haired auxiliary, she's come to attend to the neighbour behind the curtain:

'What do you think, Regitze, do you want to get up?' she says, the neighbour grumbles, there's a rustling of bedclothes, a creaking of the bed, something clatters on the bedside cabinet.

'You take your time, Regitze,' the auxiliary says, and pulls the curtain briskly aside, an abundance of flowers in many colours comes into view, in the midst of which sits Regitze on the edge of the bed, her head bent forward, greying hair falling around her neck. The auxiliary fetches a dressing gown from the cupboard by the door, stops at her mother on the way back:

'Your daughter's come, then. How lovely for you,' she says with a smile, and her mother nods and smiles too.

Palle opens the door with his shoulder, he's holding a white plastic cup in each hand:

'I couldn't remember if you take milk,' he says, and then right away, noticing Regitze's flowers:

'Oh, we forgot to bring you some.'

'Good, because I don't care for it,' her mother says.

'What, flowers?' Palle says.

'No. Not here,' her mother says.

The coffee's hot and strong and Palle has three

shortbreads with him in a serviette. They're a bit broken, he's had them in his pocket. It's dark outside now, the stainless steel vases reflect in the pane. Palle and her mother think she should stay at Palle's until her mother comes home again in a couple of days at the most. But she insists on staying on her own in the flat:

'You have to understand, I've got my things and my routines,' she says, and they both do understand, but she must promise to ring Palle if in the slightest doubt. She can always go up to Clothes Man too. Her mother asks for her bag, finds her purse and hands it to her:

'Take this. There's four hundred kroner inside.'

'What about you?'

'What would I buy?'

'You might want a magazine,' Palle says, but her mother shakes her head.

The motorway's cast in darkness, they meet only two vehicles coming the other way. They listen to a cassette compilation, take turns to guess what's next. Palle offers to stop off at E4 and see if they can get something to eat, but she prefers to go straight home.

'No thanks, we've got some chicken stew.'

'That sounds nice. I feel hungrier now,' he says.

The music begins to fade, they each have a quick guess. But the tape's run out and they don't turn it over, because Palle has to concentrate. He indicates and negotiates the bend in the slip road at the appropriate speed, looks both ways several times at the junction, even though all is dark.

'There we are, mission accomplished,' he says as he pulls out. The white lines light up the road for a bit, after that they're too worn down. But they're nearly home by then. They part company in the little car park behind Clothes Man.

Because she mentioned the chicken stew, she looks in the freezer compartment for it the minute she's back in the flat. It's on top of the bag of rhubarb from Ringsebøllevej, the rhubarb's about eighteen months old. She places the plastic box containing the stew in some hot water, and once the edges are thawed she slides the stew out into a saucepan. She heats it quickly, the peas pale. In the bedroom, her mother's bed is made and the cushions arranged the way they're supposed to be. Her clothes lie neatly folded in the wardrobe and drawers.

31

The fair-haired auxiliary's name is Belli, she wears a knitted shrug. She comes into the day room with coffee and a thick slice of cheese on a saucer, puts them both down in front of her mother.

'There's sugar in, you could do with something sweet, I'm sure,' she says, and sits down beside them. She flexes her feet, she's got sandals on, woolly socks with a bell pattern.

'You think so, do you?' her mother says.

Someone's gone from a game of Ludo at the other end of the table. Belli reaches for the dice cup, makes some noises into it. They laugh, all three. Her mother leans forward and places the cheese slice on half a bread roll.

'What about you, don't you want a roll?' Belli says.

'No thanks, I've just had my sandwiches,' she says.

'They're very good. Go on, have one,' her mother says.

'Are you on foot?' Belli says.

'Yes, just from the station though.'

'It's a good walk, nevertheless.'

'Splendid. No, scratch that,' her mother says with her mouth full, and all three of them laugh again.

One of the other auxiliaries comes in with a jug of water, makes for the mottled plant in the window.

'Good idea, Karen,' Belli says.

'I've been thinking about it for a week,' Karen says, and wipes the windowsill under the plant with her sleeve, turns to her mother:

'How are you feeling today?' she says, her mother takes a moment to finish what's in her mouth:

'I'm in the middle of a roll.'

'Won't your daughter have one? They're just baked.'

'I've already tried,' her mother says.

'No, thanks,' she says.

'Karen, can you do that one as well while you're at it?' Belli says, and indicates a cyclamen on top of the bookcase.

'I missed that completely,' Karen says.

'What a lot you have to think about,' her mother says.

Back in the room, Regitze's son has come to visit. He sits on a chair at the foot of Regitze's bed, neither of them speaks. He's a grown man with wispy hair, his hands are in his lap. He nods politely when they come in. Her mother climbs into bed, they elevate the head end as far as it goes. There's a bunch of fresh deep-red roses in a vase on the windowsill.

'That was a lovely roll,' her mother says to no one in particular.

They take the crossword from the bedside cabinet, study it in silence for some time. Eventually, her mother reaches into her sponge bag, finds a vial containing a free perfume sample and dabs both her wrists. She flaps her hands, a smell of apple spreads.

'I'm not sure I'm keen,' she says, and sniffs a wrist, asks for the head end to be lowered after all.

While her mother rests, she walks up and down the corridor. She looks at the board showing pictures of the staff, she finds Karen and Belli, there's a male nurse too, her mother talks about him. The kitchen door's open, the kitchen lady stands leaning back against the worktop with a cigarette, she waves her in:

'Do you want some roly-poly?' she says.

'No thanks.'

'You can sit here,' the kitchen lady says, she points to a table by the window. The roly-poly's on a big dish, the kitchen lady cuts a slice, tilts it over onto a plate.

'It's apricot,' she says, and puts the plate in front of her. She stubs her cigarette out in the ashtray in the windowsill, waves to someone outside.

'His hands are full down there,' she says, and waves again. After a moment, she pulls her glasses down from her forehead and starts crossing things off a list. The roly-poly's warm, the sugar crunches. Down below, a man's busy salting. A patient wearing an overcoat on top of their pyjamas emerges from a side building, proceeds cautiously along the footpath. It's getting dark, the lampposts throw islands of light into the snow.

'Are you on the bus?' the kitchen lady says.

'No, walking. From the station, that is,' she says.

'That's a fair way,' the kitchen lady says, without looking up from her list. A nurse goes past the door, but pops her head round a moment later:

'Is that roly-poly?' she says, and steps inside towards the dish.

'Yes, for the patients,' the kitchen lady says.

'Mmm,' the nurse says and cuts herself a slice, bites into it with her hand cupped under her chin:

'Goodness, that's delicious,' she says, and then, to her:

'Fru Olsen's a dab hand. She can peel ten potatoes in under a minute, too.'

'It's a long time since we peeled our own potatoes,' the kitchen lady says.

*

Her mother's awake again, Regitze's son still occupies his chair, now with a box of Mon Chéri he's in the process of opening. The cellophane crackles. He offers the box to Regitze, who takes one and unwraps it with difficulty. He offers the box to them as well, they shake their heads, her mother lifts at the same time a dismissive hand on the duvet. Regitze is heard chewing and chomping. She takes another, rustles the wrapper, the same noises repeat. Her mother tightens her lips and gestures towards the curtain, but she shakes her head, she's loath to get up and draw it. Her mother endeavours to get out of bed and do it herself, one foot's inside the duvet cover, it all looks a bit precarious. In the end she gets up after all, smiles at Regitze's son and swishes the curtain shut. It's white with blue squares. Her mother nods, shortly afterwards she picks up her crossword magazine. They look at it together. Regitze's son clears his throat.

She takes the six o'clock train to Rødby Færge, then the bus home to the flat. She settles into a seat in the middle, puts her bag beside her. Only two other passengers are on the bus. She sits looking down into the illuminated houses as they go along Havnegade, people doing the dishes or crossing the living room. The bus driver listens to schlager music. When the town peters out the white fields glow in the darkness, she imagines a bus journey lasting many hours in these surroundings. At home in the flat a straggle of clothing extends from her room into the hall, she steps over a pile of tops. There's also the long-planned sorting-through of all the recipes, for the time being they're in disarray on the dining table. She makes herself a bowl of porridge with pieces of apple in, she eats it on the settee. The telephone rings. It's Hafni wanting to come over and pick up a photocopy. She says it's inconvenient just now, she can't explain why.

'Why?' says Hafni.

'I don't think I've even got it,' she says.

Not long after, there's a knock on the door, she puts the porridge bowl carefully down on the carpet, the spoon clatters. She lies down flat on the settee. There are four knocks in all, but she stays where she is. A bit of apple lodges in her throat. She swallows and swallows. Only after a while does she slither to the kitchen and drink a glass of water. She sees what might be Palle's back, disappearing up the high street.

32

Her mother's purse is genuine leather. She puts it in a safe place, but then can't remember where. Friday morning she searches through the sock drawer, behind the books in the living room and on the shelf above the kitchen door. It's nowhere to be found, though she does unearth a dusty jar of chocolate spread. She decides she'll have some, whereupon the purse turns out to be in the tin with the crispbread. There's no more crispbread left, but they've some Dutch rusks, baked beans as well, and two tins of soup.

It's her intention not to spend any of the money, she wants to give her mother a surprise by managing without. On an impulse she tucks the purse away at the bottom of her school bag. Her school bag's always at hand, whether she's out or in. She produces her notebook and calculator, sits down at the table with some homework and the first coffee of the day. After school they're going to an opening in Stokkemarke, a painter called Schönn is exhibiting. Tove knows him from comprehensive school. Today then she's not going to the hospital, her mother doesn't see the need anyway for her to keep coming all that way, she ought rather to think of herself and for example buy a nice big pastry from the baker's. They speak the night before, she rings the payphone in the corridor. It carries on beeping in the background a while as they talk. Her mother's having meatballs in curry sauce, she sounds bright.

*

In the long break she meets up with Tove in the common room. They find a good place to sit on one of the sofas, Tove puts her feet up on the table. Grey light falls in through the basement windows, someone wipes dust off the weeping fig with a square of greaseproof from their sandwiches. They sit with a timetable, plan the trip to Stokkemarke. If Tove skips last lesson, they can catch an earlier bus. On the other hand, it leaves them with three quarters of an hour to kill before the opening. There's also the illogical option of taking the train all the way to Nakskov and then the bus in the reverse direction. They decide that Tove will stay for last lesson. They'll just have to come a bit late, but others are bound to as well. Tove puts a hand to her brow, she's got a sore throat. She wants to get a cup of hot chocolate or perhaps beef tea from the machine. She asks if she can lend her five kroner, but she can't.

'Not even a couple of ones?' Tove says.

'No, sorry,' she says.

She makes her way to chemistry with her school bag over her arm. It keeps sliding down the sleeve of her thermal jacket. It's too warm for a thermal jacket, but she's wearing it because of chemistry. They get called to the blackboard one after another according to an unfathomable system, though they note that colourful clothing heightens the risk. The thermal jacket works, she's left in peace at any rate. They're working on salts, Hafni goes to the board. She's up there nearly the whole period, her plait swings and swings.

While Tove's in her last lesson, she goes down into the common room again. A boy's asleep on a sofa, apart from him there's no one there. She sits beneath a window, pulls a book from her bag. Cars pass through the slush on the road outside, a bit later the caretaker trudges past. Every so often she looks up at the boy, he lies facing her on his side with a foot up on the arm. He's got fair hair with a parting down the middle and a broad chest. His breathing is heavy. At one point he smiles in his sleep. Then suddenly he opens his eyes and looks straight at her. She turns instantly back to her book, reads something about apartheid. She can still sense him looking at her, his face looms over the top of the book. After a suitable interval she turns the page, raises as she does a concentrated eyebrow. She decides to look up naturally at the next page-turn. But before she gets that far he clears his throat and she thinks he says:

'Are you feeling iffy?'

She lifts her gaze from the page and says:

'No, definitely not!'

But then he sits up, reaches for his coat and says:

'Apologies, in that case. Some other time, perhaps.'

It's started to thaw, there's a drizzle in the air. They walk to the station with their hoods up. The bus leaves at twenty past, so they've plenty of time. The snow that's piled along the pavements is brown and black, they tread in old foot holes. Some people they know are standing outside the station with a joss stick, they can't get it lit. Tove gets on the bus first, proceeds towards the back. She's about to follow, only the driver stops her. He says her pass isn't valid for Stokkemarke, it's only valid for her school route.

'But I've gone to Nykøbing on it lots of times,' she says.

'Then you've gone illegally. You need to buy a ticket.'

She looks down the aisle, Tove's sitting with her eyes shut, she's holding her coat closed at the throat.

'Do you mind if I just speak to my friend a second?' she says, the bus driver nods.

She hastens down to where Tove's sitting, they compare bus passes, Tove's indeed covers more zones. It's probably because she's originally from Østofte. There's a minute until the bus leaves, they don't know what to do. Tove jumps up and shouts:

'Hey!'

Another student's coming towards them, but he hasn't a penny on him, his wages haven't come through. He cleans at a care home, there's always some snag with their payments. The only other passengers are school kids with wet hair, they keep tossing a plastic bag between them. The driver starts the engine, pokes his head out and looks down the aisle at her. She goes up to him and says:

'I've got money.'

'Good.'

'But only in big notes.'

'Then you'll have to get some change and catch the next one.'

'I'll do that. Thank you very much, have a really nice day,' she says, and alights with her bag. She crosses the bus bays with shoulders straight, turns when the bus pulls away. Tove looks out open-mouthed, a hand on her head, the other student stares. She smiles at them, the corners of her mouth tremble, her heart thumps. She feels weak all the way down to her calves, goes inside and drinks some water from the tap in the station toilets. The water's warm with a sickly taste, she goes outside again, spits over by the Stiftsmuseum. There's half an hour before the next bus home. She wanders back and forth in front of the station building, until it starts raining heavily, then she goes inside into the waiting room, perches on a backrest. She doesn't previously perch on a backrest, it's normally a certain type who does.

33

Henrik Strøm's picking her up on his moped, she doesn't realise. It's parked on the pavement below with his crash helmet on the handlebar, he's standing beside it in jeans and a red anorak, he waves. She waves back and signals to him that she'll be down in two minutes. These two minutes she spends in the kitchen with her forefinger pressed to her lips. Then she turns the lights off and goes down to meet him. They both laugh. He hands her the crash helmet, helps her with the visor. He takes an after-school biology class in Rødbyhavn, he's their youngest teacher ever. He hears from someone that she's thinking of opting for natural science next year, phones and invites her to sit in. They can't really talk on the way there because of the engine noise. She holds him around the waist, the visor bumps against his back, but it doesn't seem to bother him. He pats her hand in a friendly gesture, the air inside the crash helmet is damp.

She closes her eyes. She thinks about sitting like that all the way across Møn, for instance. But summer will be nicer, they can stop along the way then and describe what they see, animals and plants. She has a wish to express herself in longer sentences. Now he pats her arm and points, someone's left a wicker chair at the side of the road.

He locks the moped using a chain lock and they walk side by side into the Havneskolen building and down a long corridor to the classroom where the biology class is taught. Four pupils have arrived already, they're eating pick and mix from the ferries, because one of them has a birthday. They're offered the bag as soon as they come through the door.

'Well, many happy returns,' he says, and puts the crash helmet down on the teacher's rostrum, takes a sweet, then passes the bag to her:

'This is my assistant,' he says, she smiles at everyone:

'Hiya,' she says.

The class has twelve pupils, everyone's there on time. She's given a seat at the front. She struggles with a chewy liquorice, but it doesn't matter. Everyone's focused on Henrik Strøm, they call him Strøm. For a long time he sits crouching on a chair in the middle of the horseshoe, he's so dedicated, talks about biotope, habitat, niche. They're going to make insect terrariums, they're well underway with the preparations. There are thousands of kinds of stick insects, not to mention spittlebugs.

She goes with him to the staff room to borrow a mug and see if anyone's left some milk in the fridge. He has coffee with him in a small thermos flask, he himself intends to drink from the screw-on cup. The light from the car park falls in through the panes and forms rectangles on the floor. He finds a carton of semi-skimmed that smells only slightly off, and hands it to her. She kisses him on the cheek with the milk in her hand, it seems to confuse him, the fridge door's wide open. But he walks close to her side all the way back to the biology room, he has a red sweater on, the same red as his anorak. Everyone returns to their seats again, they make lists of interesting insects.

They discuss whether there's a problem in biology being next door to home economics, they all laugh a lot, and one of the boys tells them about his new fishing reel. In April they're going on a trip to Falsterbo to look at migrating birds and, if they're lucky, the black woodpecker.

When there's no more time left they all join together to clear the desks and put up the chairs. The one whose birthday it is is excused, he needs to be getting home to his cake. She takes the blackboard cloth and gives the teacher's desk a somewhat dusty wipe. After that, she takes her mug and a used glass back to the staff room and washes them both while he locks up. They amble along the yellow-brick corridor, he with the crash helmet dangling from his hand. She compliments him on his teaching and the way he talks to the pupils.

'It's nothing, really,' he says.

He wrestles a bit with the moped's stand, but soon has it sorted. They wheel across the car park and up to the main road while talking about leisure interests. He and his younger brother have started turning the television on halfway through a film, then each puts forward a theory as to what's happened.

'How do you know who's right?' she says.

'That's just it,' he says, and they laugh.

She inadvertently mentions cutting things out of magazines and newspapers. He asks what newspaper they keep, and she says it depends. She turns the conversation towards interior design.

'You mean in the home?' he says.

'Yes, the home as well,' she says, but it doesn't really resonate with him, in their house things just have to work.

'Even if usually they don't,' he says, and they laugh once more.

Again she sits close against his red anorak, visor bumping, reveries of Møn. This time he goes round the back of the dairy and past the playing fields, it's longer that way, she reads things into it. But when eventually he switches the engine off on the pavement below the flat, he says:

'I think that was the police up on Kirke Allé.'

'Where?'

'Outside a house.'

'Then it's a good thing you went the other way,' she says.

She hands him the crash helmet, kisses him on the cheek a second time. The moped rolls forward a bit, he smiles and says:

'Whoa.'

Then a moment later, with an upward nod at the flat:

'You keep an early bedtime.'

'Yes, sleep well,' she says, she doesn't understand what he means until she's halfway up the stairs. But of course, she turns the lights off when he picks her up. He probably doesn't notice.

34

There are so many who are nursing colds. She wakes up early Friday morning with a terrible sore throat, staggers to the bathroom to find an aspirin. Snatches a sweater up off the floor and wraps it around her before getting back into bed. The alarm clock doesn't ring for another hour. Only it doesn't ring, or else it's her. She wakes up at quarter past twelve, with a thumping headache to boot. Her nose starts to run in the afternoon, she lies down on the settee with her duvet. There's a small problem concerning the washing, meaning she utilises each handkerchief to the full. She has the radio on, makes cocoa with water. At half past three she phones the hospital, they wheel the payphone in to her mother.

'Pet, are you poorly?' her mother says.

'No,' she says.

'Oh, what a shame. Are you eating?'

'Yes.'

'You must promise me to stay under the covers,' her mother says, and she does. She promises too to turn the radiator up and give Palle a ring. He can bring her something from the delicatessen, something she likes, roast pork or a fried fillet of fish.

'But I can't really swallow,' she says.

'Then take an aspirin. Tell him to bring you some elderberry syrup as well. And some biscuits.'

Now her mother goes quiet, the line crackles.

'Are you upset, Mum?' she says.

'No,' her mother says.

'You mustn't be upset, I'm sure I'll be all right again in the morning,' she says.

They agree that she won't come and visit before Monday at the earliest. She must stay inside and get properly well. Besides, her mother's possibly being discharged Tuesday, she's doing better now, today she's got lipstick on.

She rings Clothes Man, it's the owner who answers. Palle's with a customer, his voice can be heard in the background. While she waits, she looks up through the high street. The sales are on in many of the shops, people scamper back and forth. There's a draught from the window, she rearranges the guest towel they use to exclude it. It's camouflaged behind an oblong flower-pot holder. Then Palle comes to the phone. She says she's promised to ring and tell him he's to come with some roast pork, only she doesn't want any.

'Roast pork?' Palle says.

'Yes, or a fried fillet of fish. It's just that I've got a cold.'

'I can hear that.'

'But I'm all right, I don't need anything. I've got someone coming round tonight anyway.'

'That's nice for you.'

'It's just that I promised to ring.'

'You can ring any time, you know that. Get well soon.'

After their conversation she goes to the kitchen and opens a tin of tomato soup. As she tips it into the saucepan, she gets the idea to bake baguettes. They've got dry yeast, and there's still some eggs. She puts the saucepan to one side and prepares the dough, she'll bake double the amount and freeze the rest for later. That way they can have a cheese board one night when her mother comes home. The dough turns out perfectly elastic and releases easily, she uses it to absorb the excess flour on the worktop. She leaves it to rise by the water pipes in the bathroom. Back in the living room she halts, the recipes lie spread across the dining table, she hears herself say:

'I've just about had it with this!'

She sets about the sorting-through, it takes nearly two hours, but by then everything's just about in order, all that's left is to put them away in a binder. She moves on to her piles of clothes, most go into the wardrobe. That done, she leaves some socks to soak in the washing-up bowl, puts the bowl on top of the fridge. The water sloshes over, she might as well clean the fridge now, at least on the outside, she washes the worktop down too. Even the most absorbent dough still leaves those tacky bits behind. She also literally unscrews the whatsit from the end of the tap and puts it in some vinegar, but then she turns the tap on to wash the vinegar off her fingers and must wipe everything down again. By now it's late, the dough's on its way out onto the bathroom floor. She bakes the baguettes in two lots, six in all. Unfortunately, they're too long to go in the freezer compartment. It's also quite full as it is. She puts three baguettes aside for herself. The three others she cuts down the middle, but she has to make room in the freezer. It being January, she removes the ice cubes, and bins the bag of rhubarb.

All this activity brings her out in a sweat, her nose runs and runs. She's seriously hungry, so she cooks some quick macaroni horns in the tomato soup, carries the soup and a baguette to the dining table on a tray. She forgets something to drink, but she hasn't the energy to get up again. The macaroni horns are hard in the middle, she spits them back into the soup, eats around them. She polishes off a whole baguette. Her thirst then gets the better of her, she goes to the kitchen for a glass of water, bins the rest of the soup while she's at it. The shops are closed now, the high street's almost deserted. A lone dog-walker stands below with dog and bicycle.

She must keep awake a few hours yet. If she wakes up too early tomorrow, her Saturday will be far too long and she won't know what to do with it. Apart from washing the socks in the washing-up bowl she has no plans. Something feels amiss. She lies on the settee and listens a while, then crawls into the hall and puts her ear to the door. She opens the letter box too and peers across the landing at the stairwell's moss-green wall. Back in the living room she passes the time looking up different names in the phone book, each leads her on to the next. Her mother's listed under their previous address. Then she knows what's wrong. She goes to the kitchen again and pulls the bag of rhubarb out of the bin, it's slathered with tomato soup and macaroni horns. She rinses it and tips the rhubarb pieces into a saucepan, adds sugar, but decides to leave the rest until tomorrow. That way she'll have something else to do. She needs jam jars too, there are some under the back stairs, but she can't go down to get them yet, the bulb goes yesterday.

35

Saturday after midday she wraps up in several woolly jumpers underneath her anorak, her mother always suggests cotton wool roll or even newspapers against the chest, the latter she refuses. She trudges to Nebbelunde without working much warmth into her, turns back at the pond there. It's around freezing, her breath is white. She blows her nose by a tree at the side of the road and meets not a soul on the entire walk. But when she gets back, Steffen's standing on the square with an ice cream.

'Hey, what are you doing here?' he says.

'I live here,' she says.

'That's my mum and dad,' he says, and jabs his ice cream, his mum and dad wave from inside the car, they're eating ice cream too.

'Can you eat ice cream at this time of year?' she says.

'Yes,' he says.

She dabs underneath her nose. A small wet stain appears on her sheepskin mitten.

'We're going to a silver wedding, only we're too early,' he says.

Now the car door opens, his mother gets out ice cream first, she's in practical trousers, nods politely.

'Steffen, do you want the rest?' she says.

'No thanks,' Steffen says.

'I've only eaten from one end,' she says, but Steffen shakes his head.

They stand a moment without saying anything, they

observe his mother crossing the cobbles, she takes one last bite over by the bin.

'What are you up to?' Steffen then says.

'I'm on my way over to Tove's with these,' she says, she holds up the sheepskin mittens.

'Say hello from me,' he says.

Because she says what she says, she carries on, albeit by a circuitous route, to Tove's house. The carport is empty, Tove's at the kitchen window. She opens the door for her without a word, goes back into the kitchen. She's in on her own, working on an essay all day, it's for Danish. She's in the process of shelling an egg. There's a plate of smørrebrød on the worktop, five halves in all, among them the veterinarian's midnight morsel. A glass of milk has been poured too.

She hovers in the kitchen doorway, still with her boots on.

'I won't stop, Tove, I just thought I'd bring these back,' she says with a wave of the sheepskin mittens.

'Oh, them. Have you got a cold?' Tove says, shows her back to the door again.

They agree to drink tea together on Monday, perhaps they'll have a Fastelavn bun to go with it, Tove's seen you can already get them.

At home a carrier bag hangs from the door handle, it's full of old weeklies and throat lozenges, there are two green apples as well. She gives Palle a ring before she's even out of her anorak, but there's no answer. She takes a very long hot shower. Even the mirror in the bedroom steams up. Subsequently the moisture collects into drops. She promises herself to polish the mirror when convenient, drags her duvet into the living room, watches afternoon television. She eats one of the green apples, it stings under her nose. The bathroom door keeps banging. Later on she gets through to Palle, he's preparing the dough for a kringle, it's his brother's birthday tomorrow.

'I've got dough on the receiver now,' he says.

She tells him about her plan to make rhubarb compote, Palle thinks they should have it with chicken thighs when her mother comes home.

'Sometime next week, all being well,' he says. 'I can hear how much better she's doing.'

The telephone rings again the moment she puts the receiver down. It's Henrik Strøm asking if she wants to go for a Sunday outing to Bredfjed tomorrow. There are rumours of grey seals and he could do with getting blown about on the dike. They talk for a while, they touch on his study plans. He's moving to Copenhagen after the summer holidays, there's a basement room waiting for him at his uncle's house. But it's all still a long way off, he's not really thinking about it yet. She holds the receiver in both hands, draws patterns on the carpet with her feet. Someone shouts in the street below, she gets up.

'Who's that?' he says.

'Someone, I don't know,' she says.

They agree on mid-morning, eleven o'clock, he can pick her up the same as before.

She doesn't wash her hair during her long shower earlier on, so she does it now. She lets it air-dry, her T-shirt becomes damp at the neck. For dinner she has a kind of pancake with apple sauce, she makes them with a scarf on her head, the way her mother always does. Afterwards her hair's all wrong. She has to wet it again, this time she blow-dries it with mousse, and she puts it up, and it falls down, and then it falls down some more.

36

The grey seals turn out not to be true, but they possibly see a jelly ear on an old elder. They walk along in front of the outermost row of summer houses, everything's locked up and unoccupied, a sun lounger lies broken by a hedge. Up on the dike they have to shout to make themselves heard. Whenever he speaks, he retracts his upper lip high above his front teeth. He points to a waterfowl, turns her head the right way. They walk briskly in the direction of Kramnitze, she wonders how long they're to stay on the dike. Her nose isn't running any more, but now her sore throat's come back. She has an aspirin with her in her pocket, readies herself for quite some time to take it. As he clambers over some big rocks to retrieve a plastic bag, she pops it in her mouth and swallows. It's a challenge getting it down without water. At last they leave the dike and climb down onto beach meadow, tramp across hard tussocks, delicate ice. She swallows her spit as she goes. He gives her a hand when they come to a sizeable boggy patch, steers her around it with reasonable success. The bottom of a trouser leg however gets wet, it slaps at her ankle as she walks. They make their way back through a small wood, they follow a sandy path. He laughs at her shoes, she bats at him. His red anorak has a hood, she puts it up, pulls it towards her own. They stand face to face in the semi-darkness inside their hoods. He emits a sniggering sound. But he puts his arm around her when they walk on through the trees and along behind the dike, all the way to the car park. It's not that easy walking side by side in such terrain.

They've got the wind behind them on the moped home, his hair parts down the back of his head. She holds him tight, presses her crash-helmeted cheek to his anorak. The engine drones, she can't help but smile behind the visor. As they turn off the main road onto Vestergade, the moped slides from under them. The engine cuts out, they're both on their sides on the tarmac. She still has her arms around him. It all happens very slowly. They extricate themselves, get to their feet. She takes off the crash helmet, he rights the moped. His chin is grazed, apart from that they're unhurt. They stand on the corner a moment, dazed. He can't understand how it happens, he keeps saying sorry. A pickup turns the corner and stops, Bob winds the window down:

'Everything all right?' he says, it's his dad who's driving, they've got some old car tyres in the back.

They both nod:

'Yes, fine,' she says, Henrik Strøm says nothing, the pickup pulls away, Bob's hand waves out of the window from a green sleeve.

They wheel the moped the rest of the way home to hers, his graze comprises four small scratches. She insists he come up to have it cleansed, he makes light, but parks the moped. He keeps his anorak on in the flat, sits down on the dining chair she pulls out for him, tips his head back. It's really a very modest graze. She fetches a blob of cotton wool, wrings it out in warm water and dabs his chin. He has some rather sparse beard growth. His fringe is a bit greasy, she smooths a hand over it.

'Hang on, it's my chin that hurts,' he says with a grin.

The anorak rustles against the back of the chair, she straddles him, puts the cotton-wool blob aside on the windowsill.

'What now?' he says, grinning still, she lowers her face to his, can feel the breath from his nostrils. She attempts to pull the anorak off him, but he presses back hard against the backrest.

'Hang on a sec, hang on a sec,' he says, and a moment later, when she places her hand in the hollow beneath his cheekbone:

'I'm 2-0 down.'

He takes hold of her wrist and moves her hand down onto her thigh. They both look at that hand.

After she shows him out, he stands a moment on the landing and zips up his anorak. He says maybe they can have a ride out to Brunddragene in February sometime, she can come with him when he goes fishing with his class as well, if she likes.

'You never know,' she says with a nod, they call a couple of goodbyes as he goes down the stairs, she waves to him too from the window. She takes the cotton-wool blob out into the kitchen, hears the moped disappear along the high street. Fortune smiles on her, her sore throat does not return.

37

Now Regitze's dead, the flowers gone. Only a companion planting of ivy and a yellow miniature rose remains on the floor in the empty corner. The curtain flaps, they're airing the room. Her mother's in bed with the duvet pulled up under her chin, hair just washed. They each have a glass of squash on top of the bedside cabinet, alongside tissues, biro, glasses case. The glasses are on her mother's face, at rest on ruddy cheeks.

'That fresh air's lovely,' her mother says, and draws herself upright a tad, she extends an arm from under the duvet, picks up her glass and drinks.

But it's too cold with that arm out. The wind's from Siberia, everyone's talking about it. An hour earlier it transports her all the way from the station to the hospital, she fears the walk back already, more so because she's injured now. She stubs her toe on the door when returning with squash. She's in her stockinged feet, she takes off her boots for the sake of homeliness whenever she's here. The nail of her second toe breaks, it almost comes off. Her mother feels for her, she winces out loud:

'Oh, pet, and such a happy mood you were in,' she says.

Belli gives her a plaster, it's hard to get properly in place. In the end it's uncomfortably tight, her toe throbs.

'Do you want a morphine tablet?' her mother says.

*

There's air enough in the room at last, she hobbles over and closes the window. The curtain's the same material as the one around the bed, which is now drawn aside. The miniature rose looks a bit sad, it's hard to keep the life in a companion planting. That's what Belli says, when she appears with a pair of extra plasters. The problem is that ivy and miniature rose, and the bulbous growth that's been squeezed in at the front, require unbelievably different amounts of water. So one thing drowns and another dries out. Belli's father's formerly a gardener in Avnede, she has five sisters.

'And would you believe it, they're all auxiliary nurses,' her mother says, Belli nods:

'Apart from one, but she's a chiropodist.'

'They even have their own choir,' her mother says, Belli smiles, she stands at the foot of the bed with both hands on the rail.

Her mother reads aloud from a recipe for chicken liver with port wine, she trawls the cookery pages of the tired weeklies every mid-morning in the day room, furtively she tears the odd one out. She speaks rather a lot about the Dagmar tart, mainly because it looks so decorative. She decides to bake one and have people round for coffee when she comes home. Her next activity is scrutiny of the week's menu on the noticeboard, they go along there together arm in arm, the staff dart this way and that. Her mother puts a finger underneath boiled cod, she has a cannula in the back of her hand, her nails are long and nicely shaped.

'You have to remember I don't do a thing all day,' she says, then the kitchen lady looks out, her hair's cut short now, it suits her.

*

The payphone in the corridor rings frequently, they help out by wheeling it backwards and forwards. Her mother knows where the various rooms are, tells her which way to steer the trolley, instructs her as to where to plug in. It's only reasonable, they benefit so much themselves from the amenity on the days she isn't visiting, they're on the phone to each other both afternoon and evening. When they can think of nothing more to talk about, her mother says:

'Let's just sit and breathe a bit.'

In the event a patient comes shuffling and wants to telephone, her mother promptly initiates a new round of questions, there's always Marna and the shop, her mother wants to know if everything's looking the way it's meant to. Which of course she says it is, which it isn't.

For Marna puts yellow plastic bags over the glass heads to indicate the sale. The windows are a clutter of discontinued items, lipsticks, hairnets, tatty-looking cream tubes. The old cardboard lower body has been put out with oversized knickers on, the lucky bag reintroduced. The worst thing is there's no longer a display set of night clothes or a ring of soap bars on the floor inside the glass door after closing time. It's all just bare. She discovers it one night when she comes home on the last bus. The whole class is invited to Hafni's for mock turtle soup, it's to cement relations. They sit about the living room with their bowls, Hafni's dad tinkles at the piano. He it is too who makes the soup. After eating, they play old-fashioned games such as hot or cold and blind man's buff. In one round she gets caught, but the boy who's the blind man guesses she's someone else. She thinks she hardly says a thing all night, she goes with the others to look at the horses, but that doesn't feel right either. They have names such as Flicka and Gerd, they're settling in for the night, snorting mildly in their boxes. The stable lights shine, she's never seen anything so lonely. A group of them walk to the bus stop together afterwards. They think they hear an owl, but she doesn't know if that's why everyone stops. They must run the last bit of the way to catch the bus, they all flop down onto the seats, laugh breathlessly. She's the only one who has to continue on another bus, she waits half an hour at the station. Rain patters, everything's closed. She sees the shape of her head in the takeaway window. At one point some raucous young men appear, it doesn't bother her, she thinks: there's no more calamity left to bear. But when one of them comes towards her, her heart nevertheless thuds. Fortunately all he wants is a light, but of course she hasn't got one, and then the bus comes. The rain runs diagonally down the pane, scattered farms and small houses are lights in the dark. Without knowing why, she goes up past the shop on her way home, sees the unsightly windows and the unduly bare, completely wrong floor inside the glass door.

First you lock the door, then you switch off the ceiling lights and cash up. You bundle the notes, if there's enough to bundle, then empty the coins from the six compartments of the till. Here it's important not to use your nails, no topcoat can withstand it. You sweep a coin at a time swiftly across the counter into the palm of your hand while counting, the coins you fill into little cardboard cylinders according to denomination. The cash balance is returned to the till, you calculate total sales. The amount is noted on the cash bag, coins and notes are put inside, the bag then sealed.

Now it's time for your little round between shelves and racks. You select a nightdress or perhaps a homewear set or ten bars of hand soap of the Maja brand, if hand soaps have just been restocked. The nightdress is arranged on the floor in front of the door, for instance with a sleeve turned inwards from the elbow and the waist ruffled in. A pair of socks may be positioned below the hem, a bracelet or a headscarf similarly employed. There are so many possibilities, soaps can be arranged in countless configurations. You check then that the coffee maker's switched off and the ash tray emptied, and leave the premises through the back door, closing it firmly and rattling the handle to make sure that it's locked. Before going over to the bank with the cash bag, you stand a moment in front of the shop and consider the day's floor decoration. It happens that it's so well composed you're compelled to go back for another look after depositing the takings in the nightsafe, and in exceptional cases extend the walk home into an evening stroll.

Her mother's tired after all that trundling with the payphone, she wants to put her feet up. They walk arm in arm back to her room, Karen smiles at them from the sluice room:

'Everything all right? How's the toe?'

'Better,' she says, Karen has a stainless-steel dish in her hand, she asks if she wants to take some food home with her tonight, they've more than enough sliced meats.

'No thanks, I'm off in a minute,' she says.

'Thank you, Karen, that's very kind of you,' her

mother says, they carry on along the corridor, past the day room and into her mother's room, they leave the door open. Her mother sits up on the bed, on top of the duvet. She jiggles her feet in her saggy socks and sings, *If you're happy and you know it*, they can't help but laugh then, they laugh until they cry, it goes on for quite some time. A nurse comes by and looks in at them searchingly, her mother waves her away:

'It's nothing, it's nothing,' she says, and laughs on, dabs under her eye with a white towelling sleeve, they need the tissues too and afterwards their squash. They sit with their glasses held poised, on the point of drinking, they just need to get their breath back first. But then there's a cautious knock on the wide-open door, it's Regitze's son with his coat over his arm, his head slightly bowed:

'I'll be saying thank you, then, for everything,' he says, and lifts a feeble hand in acknowledgement, a hand that stays lifted a touch too long.

'Oh, but dear,' her mother says.

38

The next day, her toe is purple and Hafni drops out.
She switches to the educational centre in Nakskov,
she wants to go back to some friends from her old
school. It's their history teacher who announces it to
them in first lesson. The sky is black as coal above
the roof windows, the radiator pipes clunk. People
drag their winter shoes from side to side under the
chairs. They're learning about the industrial revolu-
tion, the steam engine, the blackboard's covered with
years.

At break she goes to the demountables, looks in all
the classrooms. Tove's in the last one, she's sitting on
the rostrum with a pair of knitting girls. The girls
utter polite hellos, their knitting's in brightly coloured
stripes, there are mugs on the table, various kinds of
breakfast rolls in a cardboard box.

'Do you want a rustic whole grain?' one girl says to
her, she shakes her head.

'It's Lisen's birthday,' Tove says, then straight away:
'What happened to you?'

'Congratulations, oh, that,' she says, and hobbles to
a table edge.

The problem is her socks are too thick, she's even wearing two pairs. There's nowhere near enough room for
her toe inside her boot, moreover it presses upwards
into the upper with every step. Tove and Lisen go outside to smoke, she goes with them. They go to sit down

on a bench, only it's wet. A girl in a short nylon jacket's talking in their vicinity:

'I want to lose a kilo off each thigh and two off my bum,' she says, Tove rolls her eyes. They discuss permissable student-to-teacher ratios, take turns to shiver. Soon after, the bell goes, they agree to meet up again in the long break, Tove's got cold spaghetti.

She arrives late for her next lesson, the reason being that she goes to the toilet and removes first one then the other sock from her injured foot. It helps. But as she crosses the yard it feels wrong with just one foot bare inside her boots. She's forced to go back and take the socks off her other foot too, at the same opportunity she examines herself in the mirror again. She looks like she's just woken up, her eyes are puffy, her hair flat on one side. She fluffs it up with water, it doesn't work out very well. English is well underway, the teacher pauses mid-sentence, looks at her disapprovingly. She puts her bag down by an empty chair, digs out her exercise book. She takes what are meant to be notes. Now it's rather light outside, as light as it can be in January. A lorry rumbles past, she places an erroneous e, searches a long time in her pencil case. The boy beside her prods her on the forearm, hands her an eraser. It's a small, white eraser. She erases the e, brushes away the rubbings. Puts the eraser down on his half of the desk. He picks it up again and places it halfway between them. It remains there the rest of the lesson, she has it the whole time in her field of vision. Neither of them uses it. She feels overwhelmed by tenderness on account of this eraser.

*

Several of the group are fans of fried spaghetti left-overs. But Tove prefers hers cold, she has a whole cucumber with her too. They spend the long break talking about an impending concert. Pia Raug is playing in Sakskøbing tonight, a number of them buy tickets ages ago, now it's sold out. But the rest can go anyway and chance it at the door. Besides her and Steffen there are two girls from Z. Everyone's welcome after school at someone called Johny's, they can buy wine and bread and cheese and hang out before the gig. The girls from Z aren't sure, they end up backing out when the bell goes. And when a few hours later they stand at the checkout in the Co-op with red wine and brie, Bob's paying for now, Steffen says:

'I'm going to have to backpedal on this one, folks.'

So she's the only one then who goes with the others to Johny's. She uses the walk to consider how she can put her socks back on unnoticed after they get there. But it turns out to be the kind of house where you don't have to leave your footwear by the door. His mum's baked sourdough bread, it's under a tea towel in the kitchen. They set the table with mugs and butter, they make some tea as well, save the wine for later. They laugh a lot and talk about all sorts of different things, they even touch on the future, apart from her they'll all be leavers in the summer, but none of them wants to go on to study just yet. First they want to leave home, they're thinking of starting a commune. They talk about the possibility of becoming self-sufficient, the freedom in that, Bob shakes his head.

Everyone's in high spirits from red wine and the concert coming up, they vacate the smoking compartment in convulsions of laughter, tumble along the platform in the direction of Sakskøbing's square. They wear sweaters tied around their waists, the sweaters droop down below their jackets. It's a kind of fashion, not many people know. Up on the square, they settle down a bit as they wait in the queue. She intends to ask Tove how best to slip through, but Tove's occupied, searching for her cigarettes. Perhaps she's left them on the train, but then fortunately they're in her big pocket, inside an issue of *Land og Folk*. At last the queue starts moving, they shuffle smoothly towards the theatre doors. Johny and Tove are in front of her, Tove holds her arm high in the air, she has a lit cigarette between her fingers. She proceeds with the flow, into the foyer. She actually comes close to being swept through the door into the theatre space itself, but is pulled back and aside by a V-necked woman who asks for her ticket. She smiles and shakes her head at herself, begins to rummage in her bag. She rummages and rummages. She crouches down by a table and rummages on, her toe throbs. Her mother's purse is at the bottom of her bag, along with a number of tinfoil balls. The woman comes over and says that if she's lucky there might be some uncollected tickets, she shakes her head again:

'I've got a ticket,' she says.

Everyone has just about taken their seats, it's ten to eight. The audience murmurs quietly inside, the main doors are still open to the square. A slim couple in sheepskins arrive with tousled hair, collect their tickets, hurry in.

'Those were the last ones, I'm afraid,' the woman says to her.

'I don't need a ticket. I've got a ticket, I just can't find it,' she says.

'That's annoying, but there's nothing I can do,' the woman says.

'Can I at least use the toilet?' she says, the woman nods and directs her along the corridor, then turns to an attendant who comes towards her with a candlestick.

The toilet's next to some stairs. It's occupied, so she sits down on a stair and waits. After a bit she turns her bag inside out. She takes out all her books, her pencil case, her rolled-up socks, even her mother's purse, and puts them down beside her on the stair. It's as if there really is a ticket somewhere in the depths of her bag, because she says there is. Then the toilet door opens, Pia Raug steps out, smiles at her and says:

'Right.'

She's taller than you think, and wearing a long black dress. Her hands are seemingly not quite dry, because she dabs them against the front of her dress before floating down the corridor and turning a corner. She sits for several minutes, staring in the direction she went. She looks at her things on the stair, her empty bag. It all seems strangely significant, even in the moment of utter silence before the applause rings out.

39

Rumours are going round that Henrik Strøm has hit his head and gone funny. Tove sees him in Abra Kadabra, he's standing as if in a trance at the vapour rub, he doesn't hear her until her fourth hi, then turns away without answering. So perhaps it's true. On the other hand, people are always so judgemental, Tove says, and yawns as they pass the bus station, it's catching, they both have eight lessons on Tuesdays. They cut across the lawn by the council offices, an employee is standing inside the glass door in a long overcoat, Tove waves to her.

'That was Jonna, a good person,' she says, they carry on down to Mellemtorvet, part company on the corner.

Up in the flat she dumps her bag and goes straight through to pick up the phone book. She finds his number, though she knows it already, even writes it down on a scrap of paper before ringing him up. It's his dad who answers.

'May I speak to Henrik Strøm?' she says, and regrets immediately her use of the surname, but then his dad calls out:

'Strøm! It's for you.'

Footsteps crossing floorboards, someone clears their throat, now her heart thumps, but it's his dad again:

'Just a minute.'

It sounds like something is knocked over. But no one

says anything, a door shuts. Silence a while, at last someone approaches, the receiver is picked up:

'Henrik Strøm speaking,' his completely normal, lightly rasping voice says. Someone laughs heartily in the background.

She's standing at the window, a smile escapes her. A low-slanting band of sunlight brushes the street's aerials. She doesn't know what to say, she says:

'Hello.'

'Is that you, Tine?' he says, softly and with much warmth, the line crackles, but of course it isn't, so she doesn't reply.

'Is it really you?' he says, a whisper almost.

Very deliberately she presses the receiver down into a sofa cushion, and only after a suitable length of time does she carefully hang up.

She has baked beans for tea and after that opens a tin of peaches. She browns breadcrumbs and sugar in the pan and sprinkles it on top of the peaches, it's actually a delicious dessert, she notes down the ingredients on a sheet of paper and puts it with the other recipes on the dining table. Somehow or other they've all left the pile again. Things happen with her clothes too in the course of only a single day. They migrate to every item of furniture along with dirty plates and glasses, apart from her mother's bed. She goes into the bedroom and lies down on it. The lamp in Favør's yard has come on now, the bare birch tree stands out luminously against a section of blue-black sky. She thinks she hears the sound of tinkling bracelets. But it can only be something in the street. The bedspread smells of her mother's perfumed dusting powder, she has so many to choose from, but returns always to Arpège.

That faint tinkling again, not of glass or china, perhaps something against a lamppost. Each time she's about to fall asleep she hears the sound and sees the bracelets, her mother sweeping her pencil over a crossword puzzle or scouring the sink, busy at the mirror with her hair loose at her neck, hairpins, it's almost as if she's there, and then she does fall asleep.

She doesn't put the receiver down properly, doubtless on account of emotion, for now there's a sustained knocking on the door, it's Palle, he tries to get through for hours, it's engaged every time, no one talks that long before half past seven. His duffle coat hangs open, his hands are on his hips. But then he lowers them to his sides and breaks out a smile:

'Anyway, guess what.'

It's her mother, she's being discharged tomorrow.

Palle's got off early to collect her from the hospital first thing in the afternoon.

A home help's coming from Vesterled every other day, just for the first while.

But her mother won't have any home help.

So they'll have to call it something else.

'But I can do what needs doing, no problem,' she says, they go through into the living room, Palle halts with a hand on the door frame:

'Goodness me, no,' he says.

The first thing she does when he leaves again is to empty the saucepan of rhubarb into the bin in the yard. She always hurries when down there after dark, even though the yard is illuminated by the strip lighting from A Cut Above's back room. Half the time they forget to switch it off, her mother attributes it to fumes from perm solutions. Upstairs in the flat she opens all the windows and sets about hoovering the furniture. But it's the wrong way to go about it, she needs to get her clothes out of the way first. She gathers them up in heaps as she goes along and dumps them all on her bed, leaves the hoover on in the meantime, it's not worth switching it off. By the time she's finished, the flat's freezing cold throughout. Many of the recipes have blown onto the floor, others flap in the draught. She collects them into a tall pile. She has regrets about that rhubarb again, but no, it's past that now. She does the dishes and cleans the bathroom, even wipes behind the toilet like at Annelise's and throws the cloth out afterwards to avoid future errors. She shakes the cushions, sits down on the settee with her upper lip perspiring, an ache in her left ear. She sits a minute then closes the windows, goes to the kitchen, butters herself what's meant to be her sandwiches and makes porridge in advance with water. She cleans the saucepan so that she won't have to worry about it in the morning but can leave a clean and tidy kitchen.

She turns the clothes heaps onto the floor and climbs under the duvet exhausted. Sounds and images assail her from all sides, an overgrown footpath, cartilage and gauze, wind chimes, a shelf of vapour rub. She tosses and turns, but it won't relent, every image brings with it new thoughts and vice versa, all the time she has the distinct feeling there's something she hasn't fully thought through. She follows every path, she opens every door, she acknowledges everyone who acknowledges her, but still she never gets there.

40

The pile of recipes is on the dining table. On top rests her mother's hand, her fingers drum lightly on a chicken paprika. The slender nail of the left ring finger is hereditary. Her cobalt-blue sleeve is pulled down over the wrist, she shudders, the water trickles in the radiator. The sky is bright, the sun's just behind the clouds. There's a clattering from the kitchen. Palle's fixing a bread roll each for them and they're having proper butter. Now the bus comes into view at the crossroads behind the council buildings, her mother leans forward, already smiling.

She pokes her head out of the bus before stepping off. The bench by the bus station kiosk is bare, this morning there's an almost brand-new boiler suit on it. They return to this boiler suit at various points throughout the day, concocting explanations. Tove thinks someone's packed their job in on the spot, in all likelihood due to poor working conditions. They agree to take it home with them, if it's still there. They'll take turns to wear it, it'll look good with a polo neck. She's not sure if she can see herself in that boiler suit. But fortunately it doesn't matter now. She goes past the empty bench, the man in the kiosk smiles out at her and she smiles back, this smile doesn't leave her until fifteen minutes later, and then only because she puts her mug to her lips.

*

'To think you've sorted all the recipes,' her mother says.

'But they blew off the table,' she says.

'All the same, it's a job well done,' her mother says, Palle's standing in the middle of the room with the empty coffee jug. Besides butter, they buy cream and boiled sweets on the way home, the boiled sweets are for her.

'I just *had* to bring you something home, Palle's paid for now. They're the striped ones you like,' her mother says.

They each take one, Palle has to be making tracks.

'I'll come and look in on you soon, Palle,' her mother says.

'You take things easy first,' Palle says.

'I've been taking things easy the last three weeks, I want to see how things are doing in the shop as well,' her mother says, Palle purses his lips, goes back out with the jug.

They wave to him until he's as far as the paint shop. Her mother then steps out of her shoes and drops down onto the settee, her trousers ride up above her white ankles.

'Oh, would you give me the blanket?' she says. 'How lovely the place is.'

She fetches the woolly blanket for her and then a glass of water too, she puts it on the coffee table, with a mat underneath.

'Thank you, love,' her mother says.

'Do you want me to fetch your comfy clothes?' she says, her mother shakes her head:

'No, I'll go in and get changed shortly. I just need to lie down a minute first.'

She sits down by her feet, with a corner of the

blanket. A dog barks frantically in the street, after a while its bark is succeeded by a short-lived howl.

'Aw, now its owner's come,' her mother says.

They laugh a bit, and afterwards a bit more.

'What are you laughing at?' her mother says, they laugh again. The woolly blanket bunches and bulges, the devil's ivy in the windowsill needs watering, she'll water it later and at the same time remove the dirty plate she spots behind the television. Her mother breathes in deeply:

'No,' she says on the exhalation, and then:

'Feel free to do your homework. It'll be getting on, I shouldn't wonder.'

'Not that much,' she says.

She gets up to fetch her school bag, it's in the hall. She brings it back into the living room, sits on her knees on the carpet by the settee. Now her heart begins to pound, she produces the purse from the bottom of the bag and puts it down on the coffee table.

'Oh, thank you, pet,' her mother says.

'Look inside,' she says, quite without breath, she clears her throat, puts a hand in front of her mouth, her mother takes the purse and opens it, looks down at the four hundred-krone notes, then up with a frown:

'How come?' she says, but she can't answer, her throat hurts. She clears it again, breathless still, the same hand to her mouth, the settee creaks, although her mother's lying completely still:

'Have you not spent anything?' she says.

She shakes her head.

'But what have you had to eat?' her mother says.

She points back over her shoulder with her free

hand, her mother looks in the direction of the kitchen, it's only her eyes that move. She's still lying still with the purse between her hands, then almost imperceptibly she shakes her head:

'I'm upset about that,' she says.

'There was plenty in the cupboards,' she manages to say, then jumps to her feet and darts to the kitchen, turns on the tap:

'It was a good challenge, actually,' she calls back, dries underneath her eyes, opens a drawer and rummages in it, closes it again. She takes one of the bags of half-sized baguettes from the freezer compartment and goes to the living-room door with it:

'And I baked!' she says, her mother nods, widens her eyes a tad, smiles feebly.

There are three whole unread papers. Her mother lies with the duvet and pillow on the settee, even gives the duvet a shake before reclining, indifferent all of a sudden to dust and untidiness. The dining table and kitchen are in disarray with all the things she shops for them. All four hundred kroner is to be spent, she's not to come home with a single øre. It's quite a task. She exceeds two hundred in the Co-op, but then can't bring herself to take the Co-op's items into Favør. She buys light bulbs and batteries at the electrical suppliers, and a pocket torch as well, only afterwards does the chemist's occur to her. But the money's sufficient, there's even enough for vitamin pills and plasters. She organises herself on the pavement before walking home with it all, the man from the bicycle shop shouts from across the road, says that'll give her long arms. The sun at last breaks through the clouds, shines in every shop window. She sees herself smile, such a lot of smiling, her ponytail swings.

She decides she'll make potato soup with bacon and baguette. Her mother drops off with her glasses on and the local weekly on her chest. She tiptoes over and switches the reading lamp off above her head, takes the shopping into the kitchen as quietly as she can and puts it all away before peeling the potatoes. She buys baking potatoes for convenience. Just as she's about to fry the bacon, her mother calls out. Now the reading lamp's on again, her mother's sitting up with her glasses in a raised hand.

'If I die, don't go to Hansen's undertakers, he's offering three bottles of red wine, it's contemptible,' she says.

'It's a good thing you're not going to die, then,' she says, she's anxious to get back to the frying pan, she's turned the hob on.

'Do you hear?' her mother says.

'I hear,' she says.

During the night her mother's in pain, she sits on the floor in the living room with her side against the radiator. She says not a sound, but the big button on her night shirt clatters against the radiator slats, that's how she hears her. She wakes and lies still a while, then goes in softly. Her mother looks up:

'Did I wake you?' she says faintly.

'No.'

She kneels down beside her, puts a hand on her shoulder.

'It's all right,' her mother says.

They sit without speaking. A lone car comes up the

high street and turns the corner, its headlights sweep across the ceiling.

'I think it's raining,' her mother says.

'Yes.'

She remains on her knees with her hand on her mother's shoulder, her hand rises and falls ever so slightly with each breath.

'Do you want me to get you anything?' she says, her mother shakes her head:

'I've taken a tablet. It's worst at night.'

'Good.'

'You go back to bed and get your sleep. We'll have no more of this.'

'No more of what?'

'Misery and wretchedness.'

'That's for you to decide, is it?' she says.

'Yes,' her mother says.

41

They live in Rosenparken too and in a single-storey terrace out on Ahornvej and behind the library for a bit. Here lilacs grow at the botttom of the wilderness, she picks many bunches, there aren't enough vases. Household effects are kept to a natural minimum, her mother gets rid with a ruthless hand, it's only things. She's made up a rhyme with all their addresses. Her mother covers her ears, she's wearing her silk headscarf. It's red and blue and white. It's from Sans Souci, it survives. She pulls the uppermost branches down with a rake, walks home behind a purple cloud. Other bouquets arrive by delivery or lie on steps, a steady tide through all the years.

42

When she wheels her bike out of the yard one Thursday afternoon, U.S. from her old school is standing on the opposite pavement with his own, they were in the same year together. They conduct a brief conversation from either side of the street:

'I hear you're going around half killing people,' U.S. shouts.

'Er, what?' she shouts back.

'Only joking, it's just Kasper Hjort. He's down in the dumps,' U.S. shouts, she scampers across.

'Do you know Kasper Hjort?' she says.

'No,' U.S. says, he walks alongside her up through the high street. It's hard manoeuvring two bikes in parallel on the narrow pavement among people and dogs, covered display bins. U.S. bumps his own over every shop step, he's got tracksuit bottoms on under his winter overcoat, comes straight from the sports hall.

'Did you cycle all the way?' she says, he looks at her bemusedly, now they pass the shop, she looks the other way, unfortunately not without seeing a big smiling styrofoam face. When they come to the petrol station he needs to go in to get ten kroner back that someone's borrowed, he asks if she'll wait. She stands at a distance from the petrol pumps. The air is cold, some sizeable clouds a deep dark grey. For a while now, she's been feeling these long pulls under her chest. There's something vaguely pleasurable about it, as if it presages some not unexciting turn of events. U.S. returns, they carry on walking along the pavement, halt briefly in front of the shop that sells leather goods.

'Top quality,' U.S. says of a pencil case in the window.

'I don't actually know what you're doing with yourself these days, U.S.,' she says, again he looks at her with bemusement, but then he says:

'Business college.'

And after a moment:

'In Nakskov.'

'OK,' she says, they've come to the bicycle shop now, she leans her bike up against the window, smiles a goodbye. But U.S. says he'll wait for her. She goes through the jingling door, examines fleetingly some handlebar tape, then sets out the matter of her flat front tyre.

'That's that done, then,' U.S. says when she emerges, he turns his bike around. She indicates that she's going the other way, she's not going home but carrying on towards the crossroads. He turns again and walks alongside her, bumps his bike over the last front step in the street, they come out onto Ringsebøllevej, continue walking without speaking. The light's quite unnatural now, the green-painted house almost fluorescent, she halts a moment.

'Are you going in there?' U.S. says, she shakes her head, they walk on. The pavement comes to an end, they've reached the town boundary sign. From here it's two kilometres to the woods, but she has no intentions of going that far. U.S. talks about his brother, he moves to Næstved the previous weekend, it's quite the upheaval at theirs. He's thinking of renting a bedsit in Nakskov himself. There are some that have been done up in Perlestikkergade, with private washbasins, she's not really listening to what he says. She's thinking about how to bring their walk to an end before they get all the way out to the airfield.

'It's handier too with regard to my fiancée,' U.S. says, before stopping abruptly by a field boundary:

'I'm going to get back,' he says.

The fields are black, the low trees of the hedgerow rather stooping on account of the wind from the west. He turns his bike round, mounts it halfway and draws it into the side. A car's coming from the direction of the woods.

'Thanks for the chat,' he says, and just before he sets off:

'What are you actually doing out here? You've always been a character.'

He doesn't wait for an answer, he's already away and picking up speed, his reflector tag swings from side to side. She steps back onto the verge as the car goes past, a while later further still, into the hedgerow. Something heavy takes flight from the tree right behind her and glides out across the fields, mottled white and soundless.

43

Her mother's on her own at home, tidying the contents of a ring binder. It's the big ring binder with all the documents in it that's kept in the living-room sideboard. She pulls it out onto the carpet, sits on her knees with it next to her. The sky is very dark above Acacia, but she wants to stop giving the sky so much attention. She's in her night clothes, it's something she's not comfortable with. A cloud resembles a waterfall. Her hands are in her lap with the palms turned upwards, her foot's gone to sleep. She's strongly in favour of a cursive hand. She sees now that there's an almost invisible path in the carpet from hall to kitchen, the light falls differently on the pile. This path makes her smile, she brings a hand to her cheek.

44

Tove's proposing a Fastelavn party at hers, you're to come as your former self. Instead of beating the cat out of the barrel, they'll fill a collective suitcase during the course of the evening with personal items from the past, photographs and letters, a pair of shoes perhaps. At midnight the suitcase is closed and tossed around, the contents are mingled, one person's stuff becomes another's. Patterns and habits of old are thereby accepted and released, the result is you're free.

They're sitting waiting on a bench outside the station, they miss the bus after spending too long in Irma. Tove wanders the aisles between shelves and chillers with an exotic purple fruit, in search of someone who works there who knows what it's called. Whether it's a prickly pear or a type of plum. No one has any idea, Tove doesn't want it anyway. They buy a bag of tangerines, it's one of the last, they're wrinkled and dry. They place the peel between them, some bits fall through the slats. Tove wants to dress up the room with bundles of twigs and cat masks, and she needs to get hold of a suitable suitcase. But they can still put a different spin on it and have everyone come as the person they dream of becoming.

'Help me out here,' Tove says, but she doesn't know what to pitch in with. Nor what to wear if the party goes ahead, whatever form it takes. Tove inclines mostly towards her first proposal, she's got a biker's jacket from once:

'It's ace. And my dad'll probably make us his chilli con carne,' she says.

She can't say why she gets to her feet with her peel. She walks with it clutched in her mitten, all the way to the bin on the square. Naturally, she says goodbye first:

'I forgot something. See you,' she says, Tove looks mystified, then bites into a tangerine segment.

Up on the square she sits down again on a bench, albeit briefly. She walks down in the direction of the cathedral, turns right onto the path by the lake, sits down on another bench. Here she sits a bit longer. She continues along the path, veers off by the Hotel Hvide Hus. A smell of warm liver pâté comes from the restaurant. Reaching the street, she steps under a shop canopy and stands beside a clothes rack. It's full of coats on offer in the sale, short woollen jackets, overcoats edged with fur. She cries into a hood. The shop woman appears in the doorway, acknowledges her with a nod. Back in the high street, the town appears to her to be full of people with shopping bags and cardboard boxes, black bin liners, everyone has their hands full and is steering towards something, a parked car, other people, someone stops in the midst of it all and speaks in earnest, she hears words such as *ocular migraine*. She goes down to Frellsen's the sweet shop, Nete from her class comes out with a paper bag full, smiles and offers her one. She shakes her head, it's always the first impulse, but Nete places a hand on hers and says:

'Yes, go on.'

So she takes a wine gum, and after that a marshmallow. They sit on a bench on the centre concourse, she's lost count of how many benches she's sat on now. Nete's getting her hair cut in twenty minutes, she asks a lot of questions, but tells quite a lot too. She lives in Bursø, but as a rule she cycles to school. Unfortunately, her bike appears to have been stolen. They compare calves by pulling their jeans fabric tight, they laugh as they do so.

'But why are you feeling down?' Nete says.

She doesn't know what to say in reply. Nete rustles the bag, but says nothing. The glass doors of the Co-op open and shut. A heavy vehicle pulls away outside in the street, shortly afterwards a faint smell of diesel follows, but it may be something in the sweets bag. She can't remember ever deliberating so long with an expectant person at her side.

'Because,' she then says.

Nete nods.

'I see,' she says.

They walk along the high street together, part company at the hairdresser's. Nete pretends to walk into the salon door, they laugh and wave. On the bus home she thinks: *I see, exactly*, and exactly then the driver turns on the radio, they're playing 'Bright Eyes'. It's almost too much. The furrows glisten in the fields.

45

When it comes to exercising in a living room, a free-standing dining table presents an advantage. You can cover quite a distance simply by walking around it, all you have to do is keep going. You walk at a brisk pace, occasionally arching onto your toes. You carry on until perspiration beads on the brow. You then lie down on your back, flex your feet and hands. You look out of the window, skies can vary in a thousand ways. But the sky is unimportant now. Next you turn onto your stomach, then push yourself up onto all fours. Thrust your legs back alternately a good number of times, as if to take down a standard lamp. In the course of this you'll notice dust and dirt, half a biscuit under the settee, a furry skirting board. But no one else sees the room from such an angle. You ignore it, retrieve an allsort at best, only it's not an allsort, you're too quick off the mark there.

46

Palle beckons her into Clothes Man, she's on her way home from the bus station via the high street. It looks like rain, he's standing on the pavement next to the covered racks. There aren't any customers, the owner's out somewhere in his car. She follows him through to the counter.

'What are we going to do?' he says, he jabs a finger towards the shop.

'I don't think there's anything we can do,' she says.

He jabs again, the customers are beginning to stay away, he fears the business will be stone dead by the time her mother returns. And what if she sees the state of the place now, she'll fall down on the spot.

'She's still rather weak, as you know,' he says.

He takes a clothes reach, adjusts the hang of an elevated shirt. Sighs heavily. He's got a marzipan and nougat log in the fridge, they retire to the back room to eat it between them.

'I shouldn't really,' he says, they drink some cold coffee as well, but then the owner bundles in through the back door, his arms are laden:

'Afternoon,' he says and puts everything down, commences a stain-removal procedure, there's something on his lapel.

'It's the same rigmarole every time,' he says, she doesn't know what he means or if he's talking to her, but she nods vigorously. Palle gestures and she follows him back through the shop, they part on the step.

She sees the back of Lone's head inside the shoe shop. It looks the same, but her hair is gathered in a bun. She counts how many months have passed since the summer holidays, can't believe that's all. Nothing is the way it is. They've already got sandals out too. Lone's standing at a shelf in there, she picks up a white clog. Then comes the rain, she hurries home.

They have onion soup for supper. The steam rises from their spoons, both noses run. There's cheese on toast to go with it, all four pieces are hers. Afterwards they help each other with the dishes. They don't say that much. Her mother puts her apron down, goes early to bed. She sits in the living room with her homework. She has German and physics to do, gets up for some raisins now and again. After she's finished and goes through with her bag, her mother calls out from the bedroom. She sits up in the bed, adjusts the pillows behind her back and says:

'I'd like a new settee.'

'Now?' she says.

Her mother smiles, she's having ideas about Home Dreams, but it's too much of a walk no doubt. So perhaps they can just go up to the furniture shop one day soon.

'For inspiration's sake, if nothing else, what do you say?' her mother says.

She nods, sits down on the floor with her bag. She finds a sheet of paper in it, sketches the living-room layout, and with a pair of scissors cuts all the furniture out of some card, including an extra settee. They sit with it at the bedside table for over an hour, her mother's nearly put her back out by the time they're done, but she's contented too. She keeps talking about a floral slipcover. Then the telephone rings, they can't be bothered answering. At the last minute she jumps up off the floor and dashes into the living room. But it's only Palle with a message, something about Sunday.

47

She feels almost at home in both towns now, but still not really. She knows there are two potholes in the car-park paving behind the shopping centre, the group divides naturally to avoid these potholes on their way to school. At break she walks without thinking about it through the lane to the crossing and into the baker's shop, and she brings things back for others. She distinguishes between ordinary and white poppy seeds. She recognises a particular kind of light in the sky out beyond Skimminge and knows it's because of the lake, in which there are several islets, at least one of which has a name. After school they may opt to go via the square on their way to the bus, if they've plenty of time, or if anyone wants to prove themselves in the wine shop. If the sun shines, it falls on the last little stretch before the station, and she dumps her bag routinely in the heap on the concourse while they wait.

But on the bus home the surroundings become increasingly hers, the landscape flatter, although of course you don't think about that. There's just not very much to interrupt the view. A silo at most, a forlorn fence. She gets off, traipses home, wonders if there's any spot on any pavement in all the town on which she never steps. A boy from the corner drags his feet in front of her. His mother's the most cheerful person in town. She hears a teacher of hers say so once, she repeats it when she gets home, her mother peers in surprise over her emery board, says:

'Hm.'

And carries on filing on the settee.

She stands by the window looking out, she thinks: All these feelings for fibre cement, tile, roofing felt.

She goes out to buy rugbrød and some milk for the coffee. If she can be bothered, there's a book that needs collecting, but there's no hurry. Henrik Strøm's leaning over the apples in Favør, so she swivels and makes for the library by way of the footpath behind the butcher's. She moves among the shelves, pulling out books, assembles a stack. She puts the stack to one side while she flicks through a magazine, and when she turns round it's gone. The library assistant knows nothing about it, the librarian is consulted. She too is bewildered. They search high and low without any luck. Then at the counter as the librarian stamps the book they've reserved, she spots the stack on the seat of a chair underneath a table. She must have put it there herself after which someone's tucked the chair in. She waits until the last minute, then steps across with resolve, pulls the chair out and actually borrows the books.

At home her mother's asleep on the settee with the blanket pulled up under her chin, an unfamiliar carrier bag with something in it lies folded on the coffee table. She leaves the bread and the milk in the hall and takes the books into her room, shuffles through them loosely, tosses them aside one after another. She lies face down on the bed. Her gaze bores into the carpet. Abruptly she feels unexpected anger towards this carpet. A crowbird passes the rear yard, now she rages against its cry. But hardly has it fallen silent before she wants to overturn her wardrobe. She reaches out and gives its door a forceful shove with the tips of her fingers, the door bangs shut only to fall open again at once. It's because the floor's uneven. She wants to stamp on it, but the hairdressers are underneath, a lazy hairdryer starts. She pictures Henrik Strøm by the apples, she upends the apple crate, hurls it against the wall. But it's only a cardboard crate, it all falls a bit flat.

A while later her mother calls out. It's getting dark, she's still face down on the bed with the books a clutter on the floor. The small of her back aches, and her anger has evaporated. She can hardly get up.

'Were you asleep?' her mother says when she shuffles in with her duvet, and gives up half the sofa.

'Sort of,' she says.

Her mother points at the carrier bag on the coffee table:

'Palle was here with that for you,' she says, she puts an excited hand to her mouth.

The bag turns out to contain a boiler suit. Palle gets it from his brother who works at Asik. It's the smallest size there is, but it goes all the way down to the floor when she holds it up in front of her. Her mother still has her hand in front of her mouth.

'Do you like it?' she says from behind it.

'Thanks,' she says.

'You did mention a boiler suit,' her mother says.

'Yes,' she says.

'Try it on, try it on,' her mother says, and she goes into the kitchen, divests herself of jumper and jeans and wriggles into the boiler suit. It has a concealed button closure and side pockets. Her mother springs up from the settee when she comes back in:

'Do you know, that's rather smart,' she says, and a moment later, from seated again:

'A belt would be a nice touch. A small heel will go nicely too, we've still got those pixie boots.'

The evening peters out, eventually she's alone in the living room. The boiler suit lies unfolded on the living-room floor beneath the window, she turns a sleeve inwards from the elbow. Before she goes to bed, without knowing why, she opens the flat door and pads down the stairs in her stockinged feet. She stands a while on the pavement, in the drizzle. She gets the feeling she's being watched, but she can't see anyone anywhere, not in a single window nor anywhere up the street. Her hair collects a wispy helmet of moisture.

48

She considers using shed for rear building, interlude for breather, it's all those years of crosswords. She buys a dictionary of synonyms at a jumble sale, wears it out. There are so many ways in which to walk. But a rear building is made of brick, theirs is, last year's dock plants are brown blotches at the base now. She can see that from her room. She moves the notice-board again, uses the same nails as before, and she composes a decoration of coloured pebbles and plant cuttings in the windowsill.

She bikes out to the grassland, swings round at the summer houses and takes a different route back, loses her way and ends up nearly in Errindlev. She pedals as hard as she can, headstrong in a hopeless direction, wet with sweat inside her polo neck. The theme for Tove's party has again been changed, now you're to come as who you are. She tells herself she's someone who doesn't pull up on a wrong road and turn back. Then she pulls up and turns back.

After the viaduct she wheels the bike home. The wind's behind her, her scalp gradually cools. She looks into all the houses and gardens. On one of the lawns, a poodle sits with a tennis ball in its mouth, it looks at her.

'Hello you,' she says, the dog stays very still, its eyes follow her over the top of the ball. A couple of houses on, she hears it bark exaltedly. The air feels saturated, again one of those long pulls under her chest. The day after, she lends Nete her bike indefinitely.

49

You must not be ungenerous with facial expressions or cleansing lotion, nor on the whole with anything. The twenty-four muscles of the face require daily exercise too. The eyebrows are raised and lowered, the mouth moves quickly from side to side. The nose is rotated in both directions, after which you smile as wide as you can, baring the teeth. Last comes *The Scream*, succeeded by gentle relaxation. The sequence is repeated at least five times, this after cleansing, skin tonic, night cream. Eye cream is a con, though of course you never say so. With regard to the throat, smooth always upwards. To be done morning and evening for life and all eternity, a small effort, but highly beneficial.

50

She starts leaving the living room backwards. Perhaps she finds her bus pass as she goes, puts her hands into her knitted gloves. Only when she closes the flat door behind her does she turn and run down the stairs. She slings her bag over her shoulder, powers towards the bus station with giant strides. It takes the first kilometre for everyone to get their breath back, they laugh from near-regular seats. It's already considerably lighter at a quarter past seven. Moreover, there are some very spectacular sunrises, the bus turns golden inside, interior features and backs of heads, hair. They've homework to do, of course. But there's time enough for that. At school their laughter mounts, a boisterousness erupts. After seven lessons they're overexcited and done in at the same time, hollow with fatigue. A mouthful of apple on the bus home comes with a twist of wool from her glove, she falls asleep, wakes up discombobulated, just in time to get off. She shouts a thanks and bye to the driver.

Her mother emerges into the street in her cobalt-blue set. She stands a second and collects herself, her handbag trembles. In A Cut Above a comb is poised above a head, she takes her first step. Steady as she goes, across the road and on towards Acacia. It's a public space, she concentrates on looking ahead and as far as possible smiling.

She needs some air after the bus, trudges the long way round, the path behind the doctor's takes her to the high street. Her laces come undone, she does them up outside The Knit Shop. Her school bag bumps against the pane as she swings it back over her shoulder, a customer looks out. On past the watchmaker's window, she lifts her gaze, sees the cobalt-blue set up ahead on the opposite pavement.

Her mother steers towards the curtain shop. She nearly falls against the shop front, her legs give way. She considers a flock of shower curtains, manages even to move her eyes from price tag to price tag. She lifts a hand too, as if in acknowledgement, before she carries on.

They're both closing in on the shop, approaching from either side. Marna comes out onto the step with a garish green pennant. Her mother halts. She halts too. Across the street, Palle stiffens in his doorway with a shirt. The pennant flutters. It's the only sound. Her mother straightens her shoulders and proceeds the last few steps to the front of the shop. She peers inside. Supports herself against the pane with five deliberate digits. For some time, this is how she stands. Then at last, with a measured movement, she turns and says:

'What a grand job you've done, Marna.'

They walk home arm in arm, their postures are very erect. Passing the furniture shop they momentarily turn their heads. They carry on past Acacia, across the road and round the corner. They go in through the front door, disappear from view. A bit later, the light goes on in the window.

51

Spring comes far too quickly. They sit on the step outside the station after school with their eyes closed, faces tilted towards the sun. The buses start their engines with substantial diesel sighs, group by group they get to their feet and get on.

One day she alights at Norre, long before her stop. There's barely a wind, and not much traffic. She walks along the verge and listens to skylarks and lapwings, the fields are tinged with green, but she doesn't know if it's cereal or sprouting beet-tops. It occurs to her that she's never before been so attentive to the seasons. After all, she's from the town. But now, going on the bus through the countryside every day, she sees all the little changes. It's a good walk, it makes her very thirsty. She buys some juice at the shop in Sædinge, drinks it by a fence. An elderly man's up a ladder underneath a tree, he waves to her, she lifts her mini carton.

At home her mother's in the armchair, in a posh blouse with rouge on her cheeks. The coffee table's set with a cloth and some biscuits, a cake on account of it being Friday. They eat off the serviettes. They listen to the radio and look at old notes and drawings her mother finds in the documents binder.

She offers to make the dinner, it doesn't matter what. But her mother's so full of cake, she can't even think about food. They sit in the quiet a while. Then after a bit her mother says:

'But a cauliflower gratin would be nice for tomorrow.'

'Then that's what I'll make,' she says, and scribbles at once a shopping list.

She goes to the Co-op, she buys eggs and breadcrumbs, and also a jar of honey for their tea in the evening. But they haven't any cauliflowers. She looks everywhere in fruit and veg. Eventually, she waylays the manager, it's too early in the year. Not even the English ones have arrived yet. She goes over to Favør with her shopping bag, the receipt too since they ask, but no luck there either. She sits down on the square then and wonders what to do. Bob comes over the cobbles in a pair of trainers, lifts the customary two fingers.

'What are you waiting for?' he says when he reaches her.

'A cauliflower,' she says, and explains the predicament, he places a hand on her shoulder:

'I'll have you one tomorrow morning.'

He offers to drop by with it too, but she shakes her head:

'Thanks, but no need, I'll just go over the fields.'

She wakes at first light the next morning. She gets dressed as quietly as she can and tiptoes from her room. The flat door opens and closes with a little click. The sound wakes her mother. She remains in bed for a short while, then gets herself up and into the living room.

Coming soon from Akoya

September 2026

HAFNI SAYS, Helle Helle

THE AWARD-WINNING HELLE HELLE RETURNS WITH AN EXPLORATION OF THE STRUGGLES OF SEPARATION AND THE DESIRE TO BE ANYONE BUT YOURSELF.

Hafni is getting divorced. Running away from her new reality, Hafni decides to travel across Denmark on a smørrebrød tour, taste-testing all of the best open-faced sandwiches her country has to offer.

A people pleaser at heart, Hafni's inability to say 'no' leads to one comedic predicament after the other. A month into what was meant to be a week-long trip, Hafni makes a phone call at a truckstop and starts telling the narrator about her journey: where she went, what she did, and why she has been gone for three weeks longer than expected.

Marked by Helle Helle's signature minimalist style and infused with dark humor, *Hafni Says* explores the challenges of separation, identity, ageing and shame.

Praise for *Hafni Says*

'*Hafni Says* is a radically experimental and completely unbridled book. It's a novel about crisis and downfall, about the will to live, alienation, freedom, guilt and shame, and the heavy gaze of expectation. Simply put, it's a novel about existence ... Helle Helle has long proven that her authorship can't be dismissed in a subordinate clause. Several of her novels already stand as masterpieces in Danish literature. *Hafni Says* is no exception.'
Nordic Council Literature Prize Jury Statement

'Hafni's story makes you both laugh and cry. Full of situational comedy and consummate humour keen to the quirks of language. Full of sorrow and anxiety, simultaneously conveyed and assuaged by Helle's marvellous writing ... I envy anyone who is about to read this novel.'
Politiken

'Helle Helle surpasses herself with this funny, dark and masterly novel.'
Litteratursiden

'It's easy to fall in love with Hafni.'
Dagbladet

'With this wonderful novel, Helle raises her standard from gold to platinum.'
Vårt Land

Hafni Says, **Helle Helle**

that she's getting divorced. She's pulled into a lay-by not far from Ringe. There's a field across the road, and an ancient burial mound. She might pay that burial mound a visit, if the field isn't too claggy. The beech is well into leaf now, green is the hedge of spring. When was the last time we spoke? she says, it must be thirteen years ago. Just before the millennium change. That's that straight.

She's wearing a satin jacket and suede trousers, loafers. Everything's from Sønderborg, including the fringed scarf. A far cry from the familiar fleece doggy suit. Her wispy ponytail and rather drooping eyelids, as they've become. She's not nineteen any more, no one's nineteen any more. She's been nineteen over several decades, recollecting bedsits with private kitchenette and bath, doormats, melamine mixing bowls, black polygonal dinner plates. A pine shelving unit she sawed down to size. Books bought to fill in space, English muffins from Irma on a Saturday afternoon. Watching television with the bamboo blind rolled down to avoid the detector van. Proper butter on those muffins. She'd stand in front of the mirror and study her collarbone and slender thighs, later came the flabby stomach. She says: You won't know what I'm talking about.

A bird of prey swoops. Birds of prey frighten her, she once even turned back far into some woods. You can draw eyes on a cap and wear it back to front, it's common knowledge. She apologises for forgetting to talk into the phone.

Don't stake everything on the first shared home that comes your way, Hafni says, especially if the lay-out isn't right. She remembers lying awake all night with eyes wide open before the deposit was due. A long no ought to have been vented, likewise during the proposal. That took place on the pavement outside the Imperial. They saw *Alien 3* by mistake, all that slime. She sat through the whole film with her yes that was more of a well.

She normally places a hand on the bonnet before every trip, even if it's only two kilometres, says a little prayer. But the last four weeks approximately she's kept forgetting. There have been other things to think about. She's sorry about her choppy sentences, she'll try to sound different as of now.

Anyway, the thing is that for about as long as she can remember, at least since she bought the car, she's been wanting to go on this smørrebrød tour, let's call it that, from Frederikssund via Roskilde, Ringsted, Korsør, Nyborg, Svendborg, Faaborg and Bøjden-Fynshav, to Gråsten, there to culminate in the great South Jutland cake buffet with its three times seven different kinds of cakes. Everything's been planned, the restaurants and places to stay, a string of sights along the way. Hagbards Høj, Trelleborg, Broholm, Svanninge Bakker. Long evenings with a map of Denmark and a notebook, when she wasn't falling asleep on the sofa in front of *Big Brother*. She vividly remembers Jill and Pil. The house where Herman Bang was born in Asserballe.

She says: Sorry, I'm rabbiting on. She sees a woman walk a short way along the road with a watering can, turn into a front garden and reappear empty-handed. Hafni thinks of her black- and redcurrants, can you take fruit bushes with you? A cutting from the crabapple tree. Her pop socks are too tight around the calves, the first thing she's had to do in the evenings is take them off, they leave red marks, the skin bulges over the top.

A tractor comes trundling into the field. There are many seagulls too.

Hafni says: I don't want to be me.
I want to change who I am.
I don't know how to change who I am.

Akoya Publishing
222 Kensal Road London W10 5BN

© Helle Helle, 2018
First published in Danish as *de* by Rosinante & CO

English language copyright © Martin Aitken, 2025
First published in the English language in the USA
by New Directions in 2025
First published in the English language in the UK
by Akoya Publishing Ltd in 2025

The right of Helle Helle to be identified as the
author of this work has been asserted by her
in accordance with Section 77 of the Copyright,
Designs and Patents Act 1988

The right of Martin Aitken to be identified as the
translator of this work into the English language has
been asserted by him in accordance with Section 77 of
the Copyright, Designs and Patent Act 1988

ISBN 978-1-83675-003-1

Design by Holly Titchener
Text design by Phil Cleaver
Typeset in 10/13pt Egizio URW by
Six Red Marbles UK, Thetford, Norfolk
Printed and bound in the UK by CPI Group (UK) Ltd,
Croydon, CR0 4YY

1 3 5 7 9 10 8 6 4 2

akoyapublishing.com

akoya